COUGAR CANYON

COUGAR CANYON

LUCY JANE BLEDSOE

HOLIDAY HOUSE / New York

Muchas gracias to Martha Garcia for cultural and Spanish language consultation.
Any remaining mistakes are my own.

Library of Congress Cataloging-in-Publication Data

Bledsoe, Lucy Jane.
    Cougar canyon / Lucy Jane Bledsoe—1st ed.
        p.   cm.
    Summary: After hearing that people are planning to kill a mountain lion in the
wilds near her neighborhood, thirteen-year-old Izzie decides that it is her duty to
protect the animal.
    ISBN 0-8234-1599-6 (hardcover)
    [1. Puma—Fiction. 2. Wildlife conservation—Fiction. 3. Mexican Americans—
Fiction.] I. Title.

PZ7.B6168 Cp 2001
[Fic]—dc21
                                                                2001016718

For Krista

And in memory of Dendur,
my own wild cat

ONE

When the last bell of the school year rang, everyone in my class cheered. Martin launched four paper airplanes. Francie raised her fist and chanted, "Freedom, freedom, freedom." The whole class stampeded the door.

All but me. I waited in my seat until I could get up without being trampled. Not because I wasn't excited about the beginning of summer—I *was* excited. I waited because when that bell rang, it said something totally different to me this year. Rather than saying, "Go!" as if I were toeing the line at the beginning of a race, it said, "Listen."

For what, I didn't yet know.

When everyone else was gone, I packed my knapsack and left the classroom. I walked slowly to the main entrance of the school, pushed open the door, and stepped into the clean warmth of the early June air. My cousins Marita and Eddie would be waiting for me on the sidewalk, but I didn't want to see them quite yet. I could still feel that last school bell ringing, as if the vibration had entered my arms and legs. As if, rather than an ordinary school bell, it were something wild and distant calling me.

What? What would be calling me, Izzie Ramirez of Oakland, California?

Nothing unusual ever happened to me. I knew exactly what summer would be like. Family barbecues every weekend with my aunts, Uncle Ed, and cousins. Long afternoons at the pool, where I would feel like an oaf since I'd grown nearly a foot this year. Being tall might be okay if I were good at basketball or gorgeous like a model. But I was completely uncoordinated and looked like a freak. Picture a very tall thirteen-year-old with a black bush on her head. I grew my hair this year because I was tired of it being short, but my curly hair didn't grow down, it grew *out*. Then there's my mouth, which is full of plastic. My mom, who has had crooked teeth her whole life, tells me that I'll be glad I had the braces. Ask me in a few years.

For now, I have a no-smile rule.

I looked down the long avenue, past all the buildings of Oakland, and could see a small sliver of

San Francisco Bay sparkling in the beginning-of-summer light. Then I turned and looked in the opposite direction, toward the crest of hills above the city. From down here the long ridge looked wild, one big tangle of green. I shivered, even though the sun was warm.

"Izzie!" Marita stood at the bottom of the steps, looking up at me. "Come *on*. It's summer! What are you waiting for?"

"My destiny," I called down to her.

Destiny: my doom or fortune, depending. Like a script for my life.

"Forget the big words," Marita whined in her new voice. Then she looked around to see who might be listening before she giggled and said, "Let's go see if Arturo is home. Maybe he'll take us to the mall."

"The mall," I sighed.

"What's wrong with the mall? Look, you're gonna need something to wear when you meet your destiny. Let's go get some new sandals. I saw some really cute ones the other day."

Boring.

I swung on my knapsack and joined the twins on the sidewalk. I hugged Marita, but she wiggled away, complaining that I had creased her jacket. Meanwhile Eddie was busy scowling at an earthworm squirming in his palm.

Eddie had the opposite problem from me. He was really small for his age, small and pudgy. I think he chose his big plastic glasses because they made him look older. He thought.

"What's the matter, Eddie?" Marita asked. "Disappointed school is out?"

"No, in fact, I'm not disappointed school is out," he said.

"*In fact,* he's not disappointed," Marita mimicked his teacher-like voice. She reached out and plucked off his glasses.

"Marita!" he shouted.

"Eddie, you have worm slime on the lenses. It's disgusting. Isn't it, Izzie?"

I didn't want to take sides. Ever since Marita decided to change her personality, she'd been picking on Eddie, as if he were supposed to change, too. She used to be proud of his braininess. Now his nerdiness seemed to torture her.

"Come on," I said, grabbing the glasses and handing them back to Eddie. "Let's go." I linked an arm through each of theirs, so that we were three across, taking up the whole sidewalk. That is the best part about having so many cousins—you feel like someone is looking out for you every second of the day, no matter how out-of-control your hair is or how crooked your teeth might be. It's like being on a team.

And yet, this afternoon, something felt wrong. Part of it was Marita. Suddenly, last month, when she and Eddie turned fourteen, she decided she wanted to be bubbly. So now she giggled constantly, even when nothing was funny. She acted as if she didn't have any brains. She even had a new voice, higher and babyish, though she often forgot to use it. Marita thought the personality change would help her become an actress. She already had the looks, being small and pretty, with long, thick, silky black hair. Her teeth were perfectly straight and her smile looked like a stretched-out heart. Next to her I felt like Bigfoot.

But it wasn't just Marita's new personality that made me feel separate from her that afternoon. It was something else, as well. Something about me. I wanted a change, too.

That's why I stopped when I saw the sign in the deli window that read HELP WANTED. It was as if my thoughts had been a fishing line, casting out around me. That job was my big fish. Maybe even my destiny.

"Wait for me," I told my cousins.

"What exactly are you doing, Izzie?" Eddie asked, following me into the deli.

"I said to *wait*," I whispered fiercely. "Can't you read? The sign says one student at a time."

"If you don't mind," he said, "I'd like to calculate the price difference between the deli's chips and Safeway's chips."

Marita, right on his heels, let out one of her fake titters.

Pretending I didn't know the two of them, I walked to the counter where a bald man was slicing salami. "Help you?" he asked.

"My name is Isabel Ramirez. I saw your 'help wanted' sign. I'd like to apply." The man looked at me over his glasses. He wiped his hands on a greasy towel but kept staring. I wanted to smile, but the braces might give away my age.

"Yeah? Why should I hire you?"

"One, I make a mean sandwich. Two, I got an A in math, so I'd do fine with the money. And three, I'm good with people. Very friendly."

It was a good answer, so I was surprised when he said, while looking at my cousins, "You wouldn't fit in here."

For a second I thought he meant that literally, because of my height, but then I realized that he didn't mean my size. Before I could figure out how to answer, he grumbled, "Want my advice? Start your own entrepreneurial endeavor. When I was your age, I had a thriving lemonade stand. You all expect everything to be handed to you. A little get-up-and-go would take you a whole lot farther than holding out a hand, palm up."

Once we were back out on the sidewalk, Marita asked, "What was *his* problem?"

"Excuse me," Eddie said, "but child labor laws were passed in the 1920s. He *can't* hire you. You're only thirteen."

"Thanks for the history lesson," I snapped. "Also, I do know my own age."

The deli owner didn't have to be so rude. Yet, as we walked down the sidewalk, I couldn't stop thinking about his suggestion.

Those destiny words, "doom" and "fortune," came to mind. Doom was sort of exciting in a story, but in my own life, I'd rather have fortune.

"Hold on, I need to make a phone call," I said, stopping at a pay phone and punching my cousins' number. Their oldest brother, who was going to the university in the fall, answered.

"Hey, Arturo," I said. "What's an entrepreneurial endeavor?"

"An entrepreneurial endeavor," he told me, "is a business you start yourself. Entrepreneurs see something that is needed in the marketplace and fill that need. To be an entrepreneur, you have to have a lot of drive and the ability to start things from scratch. Entrepreneurs make lots of money. And,

Izzie, money is power. Does that answer your question?"

"Yeah, that's what I thought. Thanks!"

"No problem. See you at the barbecue."

"Don't hang up!" Marita squealed.

"Bye." I hung up.

"Why'd you hang up? I wanted to ask him to take us to the mall."

"I could have answered that question," Eddie said.

Maybe my mother was an entrepreneur. She'd started her own business, Ramirez Landscaping, but she didn't seem to have a lot of drive. She did have an advanced degree in botany, the study of plants, but never wanted to be a professor or researcher. My mother loved the feel of soil on her hands and making things grow. For her, landscaping was art. Aunt Inez once said, "Your mother looks at a patch of weeds like a painter looks at a blank canvas." Mom made enough money to take care of us, but I doubted she could be called an entrepreneur.

"I have to get home," I said. "I have to make the tamales for the barbecue."

"The barbecue isn't until tomorrow," Marita said. "What's wrong with you? It's the first day of vacation. You can cook in the morning."

"In case you didn't know, tamales can take days to make. Mom and I already made the pork. Just putting them together takes a few hours. Then we have to steam them."

"As if I didn't know how," she grumbled.

Marita didn't understand because she had her life figured out. Last month she began drama and voice lessons. Eddie also had definite plans for the summer. He was going to build a lab in the basement so he could pick up where Einstein left off. So far all I had accomplished was getting too tall and growing too much hair.

But that vibrating feeling was still in my arms and legs. I was impatient to start something new, too. Maybe that deli owner had a point. And Arturo was always right.

"Money is power," I announced.

two

◈

At home, as I made toast, I tried to think of an entre-preneurial endeavor. Forget the lemonade stand. The most you could make in a day was about three dollars. Forget the paper route, too. For that, you had to get up too early. Once when I was little, I'd sold flowers to neighbors but got in trouble because it was the neighbors' flowers I had picked.

Arturo said to find something people needed. What did people need?

While waiting for more toast, I picked up Mom's newspaper. The headline read KILLER CATS ON THE PROWL IN OAKLAND.

The article told about how some people thought cougars had moved into the hills. With housing developments crowding the mountain lions out of their habitat, they were forced into our parks. However, a ranger was quoted as saying that no one had actually *seen* a mountain lion in the Oakland hills. "People get pretty hysterical," he said, "whenever the words 'mountain lion' come up. No sighting has ever been confirmed."

The picture was scary. The cougar's mouth was open, revealing four long teeth and *lots* of smaller ones. Her tongue was pulled back, as if she were in the middle of a scream, as if she were warning, "Get back!"

The phone rang, startling me. "Hello?" I managed to say into the receiver.

"Hi, honey. How was the last day of school? What are you doing at home? I called Aunt Lupe and she said you didn't go home with the twins."

"I just felt like coming here."

"Listen, I'm gonna be late. Both of today's clients wanted me to do huge amounts of maintenance. Why pay someone a landscaper's rate to mow lawns and pull weeds—work a kid could do? But it's their money. So I'll be working until around nine. Will you be okay?"

"I'll be fine," I said, still studying the picture of the cougar. The silence on the other end of the line let me know she wasn't convinced. "Mom, Aunt Lupe and Uncle Ed are four blocks away. Aunt Inez is seven blocks away. I'm *fine*."

"Okay," she sighed. "I'll be home as soon as possible. Bye, honey."

I sighed, too, wishing my mom had more drive, more get-up-and-go. She *did* work hard. And she knew everything, like how to get the soil exactly right for native plants, which flowers needed lots of shade, and which shrubs were deer-resistant. But she let her clients boss her around too much. Aunt Inez said my mom had as much business sense as Mother Teresa.

Wait. There it was. My entrepreneurial endeavor! It was so obvious I almost missed it. I dug around in my mom's desk until I found a pad of plain white paper and big marker. At the top of a sheet I wrote:

Mowing Edging Weeding

That rocked! I could call my business MEW. I worked so intently on the flyer I didn't hear the phone ring again. But I suddenly heard Marita's new girly voice on the answering machine, "Izzie. It's me. Are you there? Pick up the phone."

"Hey, cuz," I said, cradling the phone on my shoulder as I wrote at the bottom of the flyer "Call 555-8227. Ask for Isabel."

"What are you doing?" Marita asked, then tittered.

"Nothing much," I said, holding my flyer at arm's length to admire it.

"Arturo is going to drive me to the mall tomorrow morning, before the barbecue. Want to come?"

"Sure."

"Be here by eleven, okay?" Marita giggled. "Bye!"

"Bye," I said, letting the phone slide off my shoulder.

It was already six o'clock by the time I had gone to the copy store, made ten copies of my flyer, and walked over to Aunt Inez's house. It was her poker night, but where else would I find a staple gun? Aunt Inez had a room off her kitchen where she kept her "gear." It was full of balls of string, a five-year supply of toilet paper, boxes of books, every kind of office supply, about eighteen different board games, and super-size bags of cat kibble. There was even a chain saw, though I can't think of when Aunt Inez would ever need a chain saw, unless it was to clear out the tree-size weeds in her yard.

You would never guess that Aunt Inez's sister was a landscaper. Her grass was knee-high, and her two cherry trees had so many suckers shooting off their trunks they looked more like shrubs.

"Hi," I said to the women who were coming up the path with me, then squeezed in the open door ahead of them.

Aunt Inez had folded the blankets that were usually wadded on her couch and cleared the newspapers and coffee cups off the floor. She had set up a card table and put out bowls brimming with nuts and M&Ms. I scooped a handful of each just as she came out of the kitchen wearing a purple apron. Her chubby cheeks were flushed red, and her short black hair had more salt than pepper. She was carrying a platter of hot cheese-chili poppers.

"Sorry to show up on poker night, Aunt Inez," I said. "I need a staple gun."

One of Aunt Inez's lady friends shouted, "Deal her in, Inez!"

Aunt Inez raised one eyebrow. "For what *exactly* do you need a staple gun?"

"To post this," I explained, pulling one of the flyers out of my knapsack. The ladies leaned forward to have a look. "I need to make some money."

"What do you need money for?" someone asked.

"Money is power," I explained.

Aunt Inez's friends laughed as if I had cracked the funniest joke on earth.

But my aunt didn't even smile. She sat down

with a grunt and picked up my flyer to study it more carefully. "Does Ana know about this?"

"Not yet."

"You're competing with your own mother?"

"No! That's the whole point. Mom is a landscaper. Mom hates doing simple yard work. You know how she always complains about that." I made the mistake of adding, "I saw a need in the marketplace and I'm filling it."

The ladies all broke up again.

"My niece the businesswoman," Aunt Inez said to them, shaking her head. She disappeared into her room of gear and returned with a staple gun. "Don't tell your mother I had anything to do with this."

What a joke. My mother, Aunt Inez, and Aunt Lupe told each other everything. Forget keeping a secret in my family.

"Thanks, Aunt Inez," I said, filling my bib pocket with nuts and M&Ms.

"Hey," one of the ladies called out. "She's taking all the snacks."

More haw-haw-hawing. I've never heard adults laugh as much as Aunt Inez's friends. Gales of laughter followed me out the door.

I decided to post my flyer in the hills, where my mom's best clients lived. I studied a map and chose a neighborhood that was right on a direct bus route. Then I rode the bus up there and posted my flyers.

By the time I got home again, my mom was just parking her truck. She locked the back, where she kept her tools, and kissed my cheek. "Hey," she said. "It's good to see you. I'm exhausted."

The air was light blue, the way it gets at dusk in early June, and my mom smelled like spring grass. A couple of twigs were tangled in her hair, and mud was caked on the knees of her work pants.

"I'll put on water for pasta," I said as we went in the front door.

"That would be perfect. Didn't you eat at Aunt Lupe and Uncle Ed's?"

"I don't feel like eating," I said. The peanuts and M&Ms had made me sort of sick.

Later that night, as my mom soaked in the bathtub, the phone rang.

"Got it!" I yelled.

"May I speak with Isabel?" a stranger asked.

"Speaking," I said, trying to sound like an entrepreneur.

"I'm interested in your gardening services. How much do you charge?"

I hadn't thought about that! Making it up on the spot, I said, "Ten dollars an hour."

"Are you good?"

I hesitated again. What kind of question was that? Who would say no? And yet, I had never had a job before, so would it be a lie to say yes? I said, "I do my best."

"Mmm," the woman said as if she were calculating. "Well, your rates are pretty good. I guess we can give it a try and see how it works out. Can you come tomorrow?"

I could hear my mom singing as she toweled herself dry. "Tomorrow? Um, I'm not sure." There was the family barbecue, and I hadn't explained everything to my mom yet. But Arturo's words, *money is power,* marched through my head. "Yes, I can be there tomorrow."

The woman told me that her name was Sylvia Gray and gave me her address, mentioning that her property bordered Redwood Park. I promised to be there at ten. The barbecue wasn't until three, and I could finish the tamales tonight.

When Mom came downstairs in her pajamas, I was already smearing masa on the corn husks.

"We can do that tomorrow, honey."

"I might be busy tomorrow." I was on the verge of telling her about my entrepreneurial endeavor, but she launched into a long story about one of her clients. Then she said she was so tired she was going directly to bed.

Much later, after I finished assembling the tamales, I put them in the fridge. Then I stepped outside to look up at the hills above the city. It was a clear night, the sky black except for the stars. The city lights became scarcer the higher I looked, until my eyes reached the tops of the hills where there was only wilderness, protected as regional parks. At one time even *my* neighborhood was wild like that. Instead of houses and streets, there were meadows and forests. Now practically the only animals I saw in the city were raccoons, possums, and rats. But two hundred years ago there were bears, eagles, and foxes.

And cougars. I tried to picture a cougar sauntering across our backyard, an eight-foot-long tawny cat. According to the newspaper article, mountain lions had been almost extinct. Now they were making a comeback. Some people thought there were cougars living up in those hills right now, just a couple of miles from my house.

three

Sylvia Gray's house had big windows and dark brown wooden beams. A long driveway curved down to the street. On either side of the driveway were large beds of native California plants—tall spiky succulents, bushy blooming lavender, a fuzzy ground cover—in dusty greens, whites, and purples. I climbed the flagstone steps to the front door, took hold of the shiny brass ring, and knocked it against the brass plate. In a moment a tall woman opened the door.

"You must be Isabel," she said in a low voice. "My goodness, I thought you would be older."

I blurted, "Good morning, Mrs. Gray."

She tossed her head so that her bright hair swung behind her, and she smiled. "Well, I suppose that's why your rates are so low. And believe me, I need someone with reasonable rates. We've a bit of a cash flow problem at the moment. So let's try it out. What's there to keeping plants alive, anyway?"

"Actually, Mrs. Gray," I said, still standing on the porch, "there's a lot to keeping plants alive. My mother—"

"Nonsense. Come on in. And *please*. Call me Sylvia."

Sylvia Gray was much slimmer than my mom or aunts, and even though it was only ten o'clock on a Saturday morning, she was all dressed up in a lime green sundress. Her hair was like mine, a pile of curls, only auburn instead of black. She was also tall like me. Somehow, though, she looked beautiful instead of gawky. Gorgeous even.

"Sylvia!" a boy called from the back of the house. "I'm letting the dogs in. See you later."

In a second three identical tiny dogs charged toward us. Their nails clicked on the hardwood floors, sounding like a swarm of insects.

"Sophia! Ginger! Christine! Be good." Sylvia Gray crouched down to gather the dogs into her arms. She kissed each one on the nose and set them down on the white leather couch. To me, she said, "Come with me, Isabel. Let me show you the backyard."

A sparkling blue swimming pool, shaped like a giant jellybean, was surrounded by a patio made of gray flagstones. Big terra cotta pots overflowed with purple and white flowers. Along the fence to my right were deep red bougainvillea, and along the fence to my left climbing roses, in the same shade of red. Beyond the pool, where the back of the Grays' property met the forest, was a stand of giant lavender rhododendrons that were past their prime.

"Um, Mrs. Gray?"

"*Sylvia,* please."

"I only do yard work—weeding, edging, trimming, stuff like that. I mean, you have a beautiful garden. I don't really know how to—"

"Nonsense. I can see that you're a very industrious girl. I had the landscaper put in mostly native plants. They grow themselves. You'll do fine. At least until I can afford . . ."

She never finished her sentence, so I just nodded.

Luckily today's tasks weren't difficult. She wanted me to edge the lawn on the other side of the pool, pluck off all the dead rhododendron blooms, and water the roses.

"Oh, and you'll probably meet my son Charles." She took a deep breath. Then she laid a hand on my arm. "I wish he were as industrious as you are. We bought this house for him. With a pool and coach of his own, he was on his way to the Olympics."

"What happened?" I asked.

Sylvia Gray shook her head slowly. "Charles was the best diver on the state team. All the talent in the world. He says he doesn't want to dive anymore." She stepped back and said, "But why am I troubling you with all this? I talk too much."

"That's okay. I do, too!"

She smiled and said, "Then we have that in common."

"That, and curly hair, and being too tall." My big mouth again.

But Sylvia only smiled again and said, "Let me know if you need anything, Isabel. I'll be inside."

It was already hot, and a thin stream of sweat ran down my temples as I walked to the garden shed. An old wooden fence, about five feet high, separated the Grays' property from Redwood Regional Park. I peeked behind the shed and saw a small aluminum ladder propped against the fence.

I climbed the ladder, swung my behind on top of the fence, and jumped over to the other side. The terrain dropped steeply away from the fence, leading down into a dark, forested canyon. There were a couple of trails, one running along the fenceline and another angling down into the canyon.

I was just about to turn around and hoist myself back over the fence when some nearby undergrowth shivered, as if something were passing through the bushes. For once I was glad of my height. In one movement I lifted myself over and onto the ladder on the other side. Relieved, I leaned against the fence, breathing hard. Was this fence high enough to keep out whatever lived in that forest? I hurried around to the front of the shed, glad to see the sunny blue swimming pool once again.

It seemed smart to leave the rhododendron blooms, bordering that dark, shivering woods, for later. First I would water the roses close to the house.

Right then two boys, wearing swim trunks, came out of the patio door. They were a couple of years older than me. One looked like an overgrown baby, with full cheeks, puppy-dog eyes, a lopsided grin, and fine, curly brown hair. He was kind of funny-looking. But the other boy . . . the other boy had shaggy white-blond hair, a square jaw, and bright blue eyes. Marita would think he was cute. The blond boy settled on a lounge chair without even glancing my way, but the funny-looking one grinned at me.

Forgetting my braces, I accidentally smiled back.

"Here, let me have that," he said, reaching for the hose. Holding the nozzle over his head, he twirled his body as if he were in a shower. Then he put his thumb over the flow and sprayed the blond boy.

"Stop it! You soaked my towel!"

The brown-haired boy laughed too hard, like he was forcing it. He was about to spread his towel on a chair when he saw a spider and stopped, gently cupping it in his hands and carrying it to the lawn where he let it go.

"What's your name?" he asked, stretching out on the chair.

"Isabel."

"Easy Bell," in a fake Spanish accent. "Nice name."

"Isabel," I said again.

"I'm Sam."

I nodded and focused on the roses.

Sam continued, "That's Charles. He lives here."

It felt a little funny to be working while the two boys hung out. I wondered what Marita and Eddie were doing. Then I remembered. The mall! Marita and Arturo would be waiting for me *right now*. She would kill me.

I didn't worry for long, though. Marita was going to love hearing about this. The swimming pool. The boys. The money. Who would think that I'd have a more exciting summer than Marita? *And* twelve dollars and fifty cents already.

The morning went quickly. Each time I neared the pool, Sam did something funny. He would crack his toes, or scratch his armpit, or take a long, loud slurp from his soda. While clipping the last edges of the lawn, I ended up next to him. He rustled his newspaper loudly, then suddenly said, "Boo!"

"Leave her alone," Charles said, glancing shyly at me.

Sam shrugged. "It's hot. I'm going in." He threw down the newspaper and dove into the pool with a huge splash.

I noticed he'd been reading the cougar story and had circled a paragraph. So I scooted over to read that part.

"Cougars are sometimes illegally killed for the hefty sum of cash their gallbladders bring. A bear's gallbladder, which is considered to have healing powers in some cultures, is worth seven to ten thousand dollars. A cougar's gallbladder looks almost identical to that of a bear and can often be falsely sold as such."

"What are you looking at?" Sam asked.

I pretended not to have been startled by him. "I read that article about the cougars."

He snatched the newspaper away from me. "Big whoop."

"Big whoop, yourself," I answered.

"I've *seen* a mountain lion," he bragged.

Charles said, "Oh sure."

"So don't believe me. What do I care?" Then to me, "Are you the gardener?"

The way he asked the question stripped the glamour from my job. So I answered, "I'm an entrepreneur."

"Ooooo, Easy Bell's an entrepreneur!" he said. But then his tone changed. "I'm thinking of beginning my own little entrepreneurial—uh, entrepreneurial . . ."

"Endeavor," I finished for him.

"Yeah!" he said. "An entrepreneurial *endeavor*. Right, Charles?"

Charles stood up and stretched carefully, lengthening each limb, and then walked to the diving board. He stood at the base of the board for a long time.

Bugged that Charles had ignored him, Sam shouted, "Ten thousand dollars, man. We'll be rich!"

Charles took three steps to the end of the diving board, bounced hard, and hurtled himself high in the air. He tucked and rolled one and a quarter times before straightening out and entering the water like an arrow.

"You shouldn't be snooping in people's stuff," Sam told me, stuffing the newspaper under his chair.

Much later, after finishing, I found Sylvia reading a magazine on the couch. Sophia, Ginger, and

Christine were curled up next to her. She said, "Let me have a look, dear," and we went back out.

Sam jumped up from his chair. "Good afternoon, Sylvia. You look nice today."

"Oh, Sam." She laughed. "You're such a nice boy. If only Charles had your manners."

"Thank you, ma'am."

Sylvia examined the lawn's edges, searched for any remaining dead blooms, and tested the soil around the roses to make sure I had watered thoroughly. "Very nice job," she said, handing me two twenty dollar bills.

The money felt alive in my palm.

"It's good to meet another entrepreneur, Isabel," Sam said, pronouncing my name correctly in front of Sylvia. "I hope to see you again."

Stuffing the forty dollars in my pocket, I took one last look at the swimming pool. The hot midday sunlight reflected off the surface of the water, so bright and dazzling it blinded me. Touching the cash, I thought: *This* is my destiny, fortune and not doom.

four

That morning I'd written a note for my mom, who was still sleeping when I'd left the house, saying that I had a job and would fill her in when I got home for the barbecue. Coming in the house at exactly three, I knew I'd have to explain everything, and fast.

But Mom was on the phone. I overhead her saying, "I understand. Fine. No, that's fine . . . Good-bye."

When she finally hung up, she picked up my note and waved it.

"I needed a job, Mom. No one will hire a thirteen-year-old, so I started my own entrepreneurial endeavor." I gave her a flyer.

As she read the flyer, her mouth twitched. Clearly she was trying not to smile. She said, "We never discussed you working, Izzie."

"There wasn't time! I only had the idea yesterday, and I didn't get a chance to tell you about it. Who knew I would get a call from my flyer so fast."

"You're too young to work."

"Mom! I need money."

"For *what*, exactly? I buy your books, your clothes, your food—"

"Mom, money is power."

That was a big mistake. "Oh, no it is *not*, Isabel Ramirez. If you have so much spare time this summer, then I'll enroll you in summer school."

"No! Mom, *look*." I pulled the two twenties out of my pocket.

She picked up the flyer again. "MEW," she read. "Mowing. Edging. Weeding. It *should* be ROAR, for Real Ornery And Reckless. Come on. We're late for the barbecue. We'll discuss this with your aunts."

Even though they lived only four blocks away, we drove to Aunt Lupe and Uncle Ed's house because of the big pot of tamales. In the backyard Uncle Ed stood over the smoking barbecue grilling vegetables. A batch of raw hamburger patties were stacked on the table next to the grill. The four boys were sprawled on the grass playing penny poker, which they had learned from Aunt Inez. Marita sat in the shade of the big umbrella with my two aunts.

"Sorry we're late," Mom said. "I was busy losing a job, and Izzie was busy getting one."

"You lost a job?" Aunt Lupe, who worried about everyone, asked.

Mom nodded. "It's no big deal. I have plenty of work. Besides, I'm sick and tired of Sylvia Gray."

"*Who?*"

"I did a big landscaping job for the Grays a couple of years ago. In the meantime the couple is getting divorced, they have all kinds of financial problems, and they're just generally a pain the neck. I'm glad to be rid of them." Mom waved her hand as if she were shooing flies. Then she turned to me and smiled, "But the real news is Izzie's new job. Tell your aunts what you've done. I don't know *where* this girl gets her ideas."

Everyone was staring at me, waiting.

"Uh, Mom?" I squeaked.

"What's wrong?" she asked. "Since when are you shy?" She announced, "Izzie has started her own business."

"Oh, my," Aunt Lupe said.

Aunt Inez cleared her throat loudly.

"Mom, I didn't *know*!"

"Didn't know what?" Mom looked around the table. She paused at Aunt Inez, who obviously knew something she didn't.

"*What?*" Mom said again.

Aunt Inez nodded at me, hard.

"Uh, Mom, it was *me* who Sylvia Gray hired. To replace you."

There was a long silence.

"*Giiiiiiirrrrrrl,*" Marita finally said, drawing the word out to tell me I had really done it now.

"I didn't *know,*" I insisted.

My mom was speechless.

But Aunt Inez started snorting the way she does when she is trying to hold in her laughter. That got Aunt Lupe going, too, and when both of her sisters are laughing, my mom can't resist. In fact, once she got going, my mom laughed the hardest of all, stopping only to shout, "Her own mother! She's stealing clients from her own mother!"

They laughed so loud the boys put down their cards and came to see what was so funny. They listened to the story that would be told forever. *Remember the time when Izzie took a job away from her own mother? . . .*

I stood up. "I'm going to call her right now and tell her I quit."

"Sit down," my mom said. "You can have the Grays. I couldn't take another day of that insufferable family, anyway." To the others, she said, "But should I let Izzie work? She only thirteen."

Aunt Inez shrugged. "What can it hurt? Lots of kids do yard work."

"Maybe she can take on one of her cousins as a partner and to look after her," Aunt Lupe suggested, looking over her four boys.

"It's *my* job!" I said. That was the whole point. Marita had her acting and voice classes. Eddie had his lab. And Arturo, who was eighteen, Tomas, who was sixteen, and Manny, who was fifteen, all had their own summer jobs.

"Let her do it," Aunt Inez said again. "She'll learn something."

My mom looked to Uncle Ed for the final vote. He had just finished cooking the burgers and popped a piece of one into his mouth. As he began to answer, he started choking, his cheeks flaring red and his eyes filling with tears.

"Ach! Ach! Ach!" he gagged, pointing to his mouth. Then he spit it out, right onto the patio.

"Ed, for goodness sakes! What's wrong with you?" Aunt Lupe said.

"That's disgusting, Dad," Marita said.

Still unable to talk, Uncle Ed jabbed his finger toward the meat at his feet.

Arturo peeled a tiny piece of cooked hamburger off the grill and touched it to his tongue. "*Some*one spiked the burgers with a mega-dose of cayenne," he announced, nodding at Eddie.

"It was supposed to be for my brothers!" Eddie cried. "Not you, Pop! The adults never eat the burgers!"

"Oh, very funny," Tomas said. "That's very funny."

I felt like thanking Eddie. His prank took everyone's mind off my new job. After dinner I pulled Marita inside to tell her everything.

"I'm sorry about the mall today," I said once we were in her room. "I didn't know I'd have to work. But you should see the Grays' house! They have this big swimming pool, and white leather couches and a spiral staircase. Charles Gray is fifteen years old and he's almost an Olympic diver!"

"Cool," she said in a voice as flat as a board. She picked up a magazine.

"Except," I said, trying to get her interest, "he quit the diving team."

"Mm hm," Marita mumbled, without looking up.

"I made forty dollars," I said, mad that she was ignoring me. "In one day's work."

When she said nothing at all to that, I left to find Arturo, who knew that money was power. He lay on his bed, reading the university course catalogue. "Hey, Arturo. What's 'cash flow'?"

"That's a complicated question. For your purposes, it's enough to say it's how much ready money you have as opposed to money that's tied up in investments."

"What are investments?"

"Money you put into something, like a company, so that you can get some of the profits."

"What are profits?"

"Money that you clear after expenses."

"I made forty dollars on my first day at work. Is that good cash flow?"

"That's excellent cash flow, Izzie. You're on your way." Arturo answered all these questions without even looking up from the catalogue. That's how smart he was.

My mom and I left shortly after dark. On our way home, when we were stopped at a traffic light, she glanced over at me. The headlights of a passing car lit up her face. She looked tired. Maybe it was a good thing that I took a job away from her. As it was, she often worked from dawn until dusk. As she pulled out of the intersection, she said, "You know, Izzie, I'm mad at you, proud of you, and scared for you all at once."

I understood the mad and the proud, but scared?

"You need to be careful. You may be taller than lots of adults, but you're still a little girl. I'll take your aunts' advice. But you're awfully young to be working away from home."

"It's not like I joined the Peace Corps, Mom. I'm just a couple of miles away."

"How much does she want you to work?"

"Six hours a week. Monday, Wednesday, and Friday mornings, for two hours each."

"That's a lot. Inez said she would like to hire you to clean up her yard. That's enough, those two jobs."

"What about my flyer? What if I get more calls?"

"You'll have to tell them that your schedule is full."

"I'm an entrepreneur. I can't just turn down work."

"I'm not negotiating on this, Izzie. These two jobs, period. And they are only on a trial basis."

I folded my arms across my chest. "Well, I don't think Mrs. Gray is insufferable. She's beautiful. And Charles is an Olympic diver."

Mom gave me a sharp look.

"Okay, used to be in training to be an Olympic diver. But I *like* them."

As she pulled the truck in front of our house, Mom said, "Listen, Izzie. Charles may have good qualities. I feel bad for him. His mother and father are having difficulties, and his mother puts a lot of pressure on him. But he seems spoiled to me. They're not the kind of people you should be spending time with.

"So, Izzie. Pull their weeds. Fine. But you're not to hang around socially with anyone you meet there. Do you understand?"

"As if."

"Izzie, this is not a time for sarcasm."

"Mom, aren't you overreacting a little? What trouble could I get into in the Grays' backyard?"

"You tell me."

"None. None whatsoever."

"Good," Mom said, getting out of the car. "That's exactly what I want to hear."

five

◆

On Sunday I called Marita three times. The first time she was too busy to talk. The second time Eddie said she had gone to the mall with someone named Sasha. And the third time she was still at the mall. I left a message for her to call me when she got home, but she didn't. I ended up spending the afternoon helping Mom clean the house.

On Monday morning I rode the bus up to the Grays' house.

"Oh, Isabel, dear. Come in quickly. There is so much to do." Mrs. Gray wore a hot pink silk tank top and white cotton pants. "I'm having a get-together tonight—actually, it's an emergency neighborhood meeting—and there is so much to do. I need you to help me around the house. For starters, everything must be cleaned. I'll pay your usual rate, of course."

Wait a minute, I thought. *MEW was my business: mowing, edging, weeding.* The W could stand for watering, so I was willing to do that, any yard work, really. But housework? I spent most of yesterday cleaning house.

What would an entrepreneur do? I had to think fast. Money was money. Did it really matter how I made it? After all, Mom hadn't paid me a cent for cleaning our house. Today I would get ten dollars an hour.

"Sure, okay," I said, trying to sound cheerful.

A few hours later I regretted it. All morning long Sylvia Gray had me vacuuming, dusting, mopping, washing dishes, and even making party sandwiches and baking cookies. Hours past the time I was supposed to go home, I pulled the last tin of chocolate chip cookies out of the oven and scraped them onto paper towels on the kitchen table. Then I tried one, since I hadn't brought a lunch. The melted chocolate tasted delicious. I ate another.

My mouth was full of cookie when Sam and Charles walked into the kitchen.

"She's stealing food!" Sam said loudly.

I stopped chewing.

"Just kidding, Easy Bell. How's it going? So now you're the housekeeper instead of the gardener."

I swallowed and said, "Just for today," taking another cookie to prove he couldn't bully me.

"You're lucky," Sam said, whapping Charles in the stomach. "Having a maid and everything."

"I'm not a maid."

Sam laughed, then knelt down to pet the dogs, scratching gently behind their ears and along each of their spines.

"Hi, Isabel," Charles said, tossing blond hair out of his eyes. He was still too shy to look at me directly.

The boys sat at the kitchen table and ate the cookies, one right after another, as if they were potato chips. Charles started to feed a cookie to one of the dogs, but Sam grabbed his arm. "Don't," he said. "Chocolate is bad for dogs."

"Fine," Charles said, letting them out so they wouldn't keep begging.

"Hey, I have something to show you," Sam said, placing a piece of newspaper on top of some of the hot cookies. "Did you see the paper yesterday?"

I shook my head, watching the cookie grease seep into the newsprint. It was another article about mountain lions.

"Charles!" Sylvia called from another room.

Charles ignored his mother.

A moment later she burst into the kitchen. "Where are my babies?"

"I let them out," Charles said. "What's the big deal?"

"The mountain lion, Charles," Sam said quietly. Then, "I'm sure they're fine, Mrs. Gray. I'll help you bring them in."

Sam followed Sylvia out the back door. Charles rolled his eyes and ate another cookie.

"The mountain lion?" I asked.

"A mountain lion chased a kid on his bicycle on Saturday," Charles said, nodding toward the article. "On the fire trail a quarter-mile from here. Everyone's really upset. A mountain lion could kill someone."

I asked, "Were you really going to go to the Olympics?"

His face turned pale. "Who told you that?"

"Your mother."

He shrugged and ate another cookie.

"What a scare!" Sylvia returned to the kitchen with a dog under each arm. Sam was cuddling the third.

"Absolutely terrifying," Charles said in a deadpan voice. "Muffy, Fluffy, and Puffball would have been perfect appetizers for the mountain lion."

"You know their names, Charles. Please use them." Sylvia kissed the noses of her dogs and set them on the floor.

Charles stuffed another cookie in his mouth.

Sylvia Gray sighed, but she poured two glasses of milk for the boys. Then she said to me, "They've devoured the cookies. Do you mind making another batch?"

"I'm sorry, Mrs. Gray," Sam exclaimed. "We shouldn't have eaten so many."

"Oh, that's all right," Sylvia Gray said, ruffling his curls. "Isabel can bake some more."

I was planning on meeting my cousins at the public pool at four o'clock today. But ten dollars an hour for baking cookies was a pretty good deal. "Okay," I said, and got the flour, chocolate chips, and sugar back out of the cupboards.

"So, Easy Bell," Sam said after Sylvia left the kitchen.

"Her name is Isabel," Charles said softly.

"Easy Bell has a sense of humor, don't you?"

I dumped the flour into a bowl.

"Listen to this," Sam continued. "You asked how I knew there were mountain lions up here. Here's proof." Sam read the beginning of the article out loud. "'Brian Wideman, thirteen, was riding his bike on a fire trail in Redwood Park when he noticed movement in the brush beside the trail. He only heard the predator at first, but Wideman thinks he saw a big long tail flick up through the undergrowth. He rode his bike as fast as he could and didn't look back. However, he heard the cougar pursuing him.

"'According to residents of the nearby Oakland hills neighborhood, this cougar sighting constitutes grounds for obtaining a depredation permit to rid the residents of the public danger. Vicious and ruthless, these meat-eaters are known to kill for sport.

"'However, mountain lion protectors believe that' . . . blah, blah, blah," Sam finished, cutting off whatever it was that the mountain lion protectors had to say. He folded the article and shoved it back in his pocket.

"Bob Durant said we'd get that depredation permit tonight, no problem," Charles said.

"A depredation permit," Sam spoke slowly to me, "is a permit issued by the Department of Fish and Game that allows you to kill a wild animal that has threatened human life or property."

"I know." I carried the bowl of cookie dough to the kitchen table to spoon it onto the tin sheets.

"So if you're so smart, Easy Bell, who do you think is going to sack the cougar?"

"Who?" I asked, my curiosity getting the better of my anger.

He just laughed and sauntered toward the patio door. He called over his shoulder, into the living room, "Nice to see you, Mrs. Gray. Thank you for the delicious cookies."

"Oh, you're welcome, Sam," she called back.

Charles rolled his eyes again and followed his friend out the patio door.

A moment later I heard a big splash as they jumped into the pool. As I waited for the cookies to bake, I stood at the patio door. Sam was lying in the sun. Charles was climbing the ladder of the diving board. When he reached the top, he paused, standing with his legs together and his eyes closed. His chest rose and fell as he took two deep breaths. Then he walked slowly forward on the board. As he leaped he raised his arms and tilted back his head. An instant later, he was a human ball, hovering over the blue pool, his blond hair flying beneath his ears. At the last second he straightened out and entered the water feet first without seeming to even break the surface. He came up for air, climbed out of the pool, and dove again.

Then again and again. Charles dove the way my Uncle Ed prayed, with total concentration.

Sylvia came up behind me and sighed loudly. "So much wasted talent."

"Is the meeting tonight about the mountain lion?" I asked.

"Yes. A man from the Department of Fish and Game is coming. It's terrifying, don't you think? A cougar prowling around out there."

"Do you mind . . . do you think it would be all right if I came to the meeting?"

The phone rang. I waited as Sylvia said, "But Bill, it's the neighborhood meeting tonight. The man from the department of Fish and Game will be here. Well, no, I *won't* understand if you're late. Bill, you're *always* late. So *what* that you called." She hung up without saying good-bye and headed for the spiral staircase. Seeing that I hadn't left yet, she said, "Isabel, if you want to come to the meeting, fine."

"Thank you! Would it be okay if I ate a couple of the sandwiches I made?"

Sylvia smiled. "Please, dear, help yourself to anything you like when you're here." She disappeared up the stairs.

Mom wouldn't be home until late. I called her anyway and left a message. Then I wrapped a couple of the party sandwiches and some cookies in a paper towel, put them in my knapsack, and went out to the pool. Both Sam and Charles were lying in the sun with their eyes closed. They didn't even hear me walk past. I ducked behind the garden shed and climbed the ladder into Redwood Regional Park.

I wasn't afraid of a cougar. The first article had said that people almost never saw them, that the big wild cats were only interested in deer, anyway.

After five steps down the trail leading into the canyon, I stopped and listened. Nothing. Ten more steps. Now that my eyes had adjusted, the forest didn't look quite so dark. Another ten steps, then twenty. Before long I had reached the creek at the bottom and sat on a big flat rock, watching the water bubble past me. I wondered if this creek ran all the way to San Francisco Bay before it emptied into the ocean.

Since there were another forty-five minutes before the meeting began, I started climbing the hill on the other side of the canyon. Soon I reached a grove of redwoods. Among the redwoods was a little shelf where the ground flattened out for a bit before it pitched steeply uphill again. I stood, catching my breath, and looked around.

There were no cougars in sight. But tucked in behind a couple of the bigger trees, stood a dirty, tattered blue tent. I squatted next to the door, took hold of the zipper, and pulled the flap open. Inside the tent someone had stashed a red sweatshirt, a sleeping bag, and several plastic containers. One held Oreo cookies, another was half-full of what looked like birdseed, and the third was full of mixed nuts. I climbed back out of the tent, wondering whose hideaway I'd stumbled upon. Behind the tent a birdfeeder hung from a low branch of a redwood. A squirrel was trying to reach the birdseed but kept slipping off the feeder. A blue jay circled, squawking at the squirrel, warning it away.

A breeze ruffled through the forest. I shivered and glanced around quickly. I felt a . . . presence. Almost as if I were being watched. Not that I was scared. But it was time to return to the Grays' anyway. I rushed back.

The boys had left. The swimming pool was as still and blue as the late afternoon sky. Seeing the place empty gave me a funny feeling. All the beautiful things were still there—the blue water, the terracotta pots overflowing with flowers, the cushioned lounge chairs—and yet, everything was a little too quiet. Maybe it was just the time of day, that moment when it is both late afternoon and also early evening. Like the very end of one breath before you begin to take in another one.

Maybe, I thought, I should just go home.

But I didn't. I stayed and went to the cougar meeting.

Six

◆

I sat in a corner, hoping to blend in. There was no hope of that. Besides being a stranger, I was hard to miss with my height, my out-of-control hair, the plastic on my teeth. People glanced at me. They must have been wondering, *Who is she?*

"These cookies are delicious!" a neighbor said to Sylvia. "You're a wonderful baker."

"An old family recipe," Sylvia said, winking at me. "My friend Isabel made them."

Tonight she wore a silvery sheath dress and matching silver sandals, though everyone else wore shorts or jeans. She moved as if *her* height were a *plus*, like she was some kind of long-legged forest creature. When she introduced the man from the Department of Fish and Game, he glanced at his watch and said, "We should get started as soon as possible, Mrs. Gray."

"*Sylvia,* please," she said, tossing her head. How did she make her unruly hair look like a mane rather than a mop?

The man from the Department of Fish and Game wore his uniform, green trousers and a green jacket with a badge. His face was red, as if he had just shaved and scrubbed, and his thinning blond hair was combed straight back. He looked like a big parrot because his mouth was so small under his big, curved nose.

"Good evening, folks. Uh, hello, folks. GOOD EVENING." The guy had trouble raising his voice. "Folks!" he repeated. "Can we start the meeting? We have only an hour."

"I have all night," said a thin man carrying a newborn baby. He lowered himself carefully onto the couch next to me. "Who's going to put a time limit on discussing the safety of our children? I'm Bob Durant, by the way. We moved to Fir Street last month." He nodded across the room to his wife.

Several others took seats. Charles and Sam sat on the floor, their backs to the wall. Sam held one of Sylvia's dogs on his lap, and the other two waited for attention from him.

"Well, uh, usually we try to limit these meetings to an hour," the Fish and Game man said, glancing again at his watch. "My name is James O'Donnell. We're here to discuss the alleged mountain lion—"

"Alleged, my foot," said Bob Durant. "That killer is prowling outside this very moment. I'd bet my life he's within a mile of here."

"Or she," I said.

"Has anyone *seen* the cat?" asked Mr. O'Donnell.

"I saw one in my backyard, just last night," a chubby, blond woman announced.

"What did it look like?" asked Mr. O'Donnell, scooting forward in his chair.

"Big. Had to be a cougar. Maybe four feet long."

A woman with curly gray hair, wearing an embroidered dress, sighed loudly and said, "Cougars are much bigger than that."

"Excuse me, Alice," said the chubby, blond woman. "But I know what I saw."

"I'm worried about my dogs," said Mrs. Gray. "I've heard the cats yowling in the woods at night. Sounds like a dozen or more."

"Well, ma'am," said Mr. O'Donnell. "Mountain lions have very big ranges, up to one hundred square miles for the males, sixty for the females. They are extremely territorial. There is not likely to be more than one, two at the very most, in all of Redwood Park. *If there are any.* With the death of that jogger several months ago, people have been very scared. And understandably. Yet, the chances of that happening again are so slim—"

"Excuse me," interrupted a muscular man who wore his shirt sleeves rolled high above his elbows. "But my son was *chased* by a cougar. I don't give a hoot about what the chances are. This was my *son.* It's the job of your department to rid our neighborhoods of dangerous animals. Am I correct?"

"Well—"

"And cougars are dangerous, correct?"

"You see—"

"Then I suggest you people get on this, because if *you* don't, we'll have to take matters into our own hands." The man looked around the room for support.

The woman with curly gray hair said, "Seth, I don't really think threats are necessary."

Seth folded his arms and sat back. "I don't mean any disrespect," he said to Mr. O'Donnell. "But if you have children, you might understand my feelings."

"I do have children," Mr. O'Donnell said. "And I do understand your feelings. Could your son tell us exactly what happened?"

"It's all right here in this newspaper story," said Bob Durant.

"You can't believe half of what you read in the newspaper, though," I quoted Aunt Inez.

Seth grabbed the boy sitting next to him on the couch and placed him on his feet. "This is my son," he said. "Brian Wideman."

The redheaded boy had splotchy freckles all over his face and arms. He seemed scared. His father poked him in the back. "Speak up, Brian. Tell the man what happened."

Brian whispered, "I was riding my mountain bike on the north ridge fire trail and heard something in the bushes."

"He heard a cougar," his father said.

Mr. O'Donnell asked, "Did you see anything?"

"Um."

"Sure he did. Tell him about the cougar you saw."

The boy said, "Um," again, so the father took over, telling the same story that appeared in the newspaper.

When he finished, Mr. O'Donnell asked Brian, "Is that all correct?"

Brian nodded.

"I'm sorry, but—" The gray-haired lady shook her head. "That story doesn't really constitute proof there is a cougar. I'm not sure that Brian actually *saw* a cougar. He only says he heard it. It could have been a deer, a coyote, anything."

Everyone looked at Brian.

"Tell them what you saw," his father prompted.

"I saw a cougar," he whispered again.

The woman said, "Even if he had, I'm just not comfortable with shooting an animal that hasn't done anyone any harm. Nor am I comfortable with the idea of a bunch of armed guys roaming around Redwood Park. That sounds more dangerous to me than a cougar, frankly."

"Oh, I get it," Bob Durant said. "You want to wait until a young child is dragged from his sandbox. Then we'll have proof that the cat is a killer. Well, I'll tell you right now, I'm not willing to take that risk."

"But that's the point," the woman countered. "What exactly is the risk? The facts are, bee stings have killed more people than cougars have. Dog bites have killed more people than cougars have. For that matter, *deer kicks* have killed more people than cougars have. Shall we hunt down all the bees, dogs, and deer?"

"She's right," said a potbellied man wearing half-glasses. "*If*, and it's a big if, there are any cougars in Redwood Park, they were here before we were. We can't just wipe out whatever gets in our way."

"Look," said Seth. "We're not talking about raccoons getting into our garbage cans at night. We're talking about major predators." He turned to speak directly to O'Donnell. "I'm sorry, but this just isn't a time to coddle animal lovers. We have to take action."

"But we're animals, too," I said. "And besides, the cougars eat deer, not people. The deer population up here is exploding. So even if there were a cougar up here, it would eat the deer, not the people."

Everyone looked at me. Of course, their suspicious stares didn't stop big-mouthed me. I said, "God made all the animals and put us together on earth. Why should we harm one that hasn't harmed us?"

"A wise girl," said the gray-haired woman.

"I'll second that," said the potbellied man.

Brian's father placed his elbows on his knees and leaned toward me. "You cannot compare these animals to humans. The cougars are not rational. They're killers. Have you ever seen the way they mangle their prey? Let me tell you, young lady, it isn't pretty."

"Oh my," said Sylvia.

"I'm afraid we haven't met," Mr. Durant said to me. "Where exactly is your home?"

"You don't know Isabel?" Sam asked the group, as if not knowing me was a big mistake. "Isabel is a friend of Charles's and mine. She knows a lot about cougars."

He sounded as if he liked me!

"What we need now," Seth said, "is to get that depredation permit. So if Mr. O'Donnell will just issue it, we can all go home feeling a whole lot safer. It'll be a dirty job, but someone has to do it, so I'm willing to help arrange for the disposal of the cat. Shall we make a committee?"

"Thank you all for your input," Mr. O'Donnell said. "I appreciate your concern and the information you have shared with me. However, I need to do further research before deciding about issuing a depredation permit. And *if* my department issues one, *we* will handle the removal of the cat. There are many options. Capturing the animal and relocating him is one. But first I have to look into this much more thoroughly. I'll let you know my decision in, say, a week's time. How does that sound?"

"Ha!" shouted Bob Durant. His baby squawked, too. "A week may be too late. Like Seth said, I'm just not willing to take the risk." The baby started screaming, her face reddening.

"I'm sorry, sir," Mr. O'Donnell said, trying to speak over the baby's crying, "but there is a procedure and we will follow it. Good night, everyone."

On my way to the bus stop, I passed a small group of men from the meeting on the street. They were leaning against a car. Sam sat on the hood of the car, listening. They hushed as I passed, but I heard one of them say, "There really is no other choice."

Seven

On Thursday I began working at Aunt Inez's. "You'll need a backhoe for that yard," my mom had said when I left in the morning, and she was right. The weeds were now waist high.

"It's the entrepreneur," Aunt Inez greeted me at the door. "Ana tells me you're raking in the dough. Let me know when I can retire."

"Not yet."

"Well, what about a job? How much would you pay me if I worked for you?"

"As if. I'm here to work for *you*."

"Okay, okay. But when you hit the big time, don't forget who was there for you at the start."

"I won't. Can I have one of these?" I hefted a bag of donuts off her kitchen counter.

"Just one. Those are for a meeting at work this morning."

I took a maple bar and a chocolate donut, then poured myself a glass of milk. Aunt Inez was using a sticky roller to get the cat hairs off her blouse. Her two cats, Virginia and Nicholas, wove in and out between her legs, so she had to roll her pant legs, too.

"It's a losing battle," she said. "Since it's gotten so hot, they're shedding like crazy."

Virginia, an orange tabby, and Nicholas, a black and white tuxedo cat, looked innocent. They purred and came over to rub against my legs as well. I tried to picture each of them about ten times their size. They still wouldn't look very scary.

"Hey, Aunt Inez, some people say there might be a cougar living in Redwood Park. Do you think that's possible?"

"It's possible."

"But do you think it is really there?"

"Wouldn't surprise me."

"Okay, if there is a cougar up in the hills, do you think it should be killed?"

Aunt Inez bent to pet her cats one last time before leaving for work. Then she picked up the bag of donuts and her purse. "Why would you *kill* it?"

"If it was a danger to people living in the neighborhoods next to Redwood Park. Like, what if a cougar dragged a young child from his or her sandbox?"

"That sounds gruesome. I gotta go. My meeting started fifteen minutes ago."

"Aunt Inez, you're gonna get fired!"

"They can't fire me. I'm the boss. See you later. Hey, I expect a yard full of blooming posies when I get home tonight."

"As if. It'll take me a few days just to get to where we can see the soil."

Whacking Aunt Inez's weeds went slowly because the cats kept following me around and I didn't want to hit them with the weed whacker. They must have been upset because I was destroying their mouse hunting grounds.

Virginia caught two mice that morning and spent a lot of time batting them around before killing them. It made me think about what the newspaper article said: Cougars kill just for sport. Virginia did seem to have fun playing with the captured mice.

Nicholas spent most of his time pacing on the fence tops. Sometimes he would pounce into the yard, as if he were attacking something, but he never caught anything.

That afternoon I went to the library and checked out several books on cougars. I spent the rest of the week reading them. By Sunday I had a lot of information and also a lot of questions. We were going over to Aunt Lupe and Uncle Ed's house for another barbecue, which made me glad, because I hadn't seen Marita all week. Also I hoped that my cousins would help me figure out what to do about the cougar.

Uncle Ed was just firing up the coals when we arrived. "Your cousins are in the basement," he told me. "I think they're looking up baseball statistics on the Net."

Their hooting could be heard from the upstairs hallway. It was unlikely they were hooting about baseball statistics. When I reached the bottom of the stairs, the three older boys were slapping each other's hands in high fives. Only Eddie wasn't laughing. He stood, scowling furiously, in front of the door to the linen closet he had converted into a lab.

"That's not funny," Marita said. "It's *disgusting.* You guys make me sick."

"Wait, wait, wait!" Manny shushed his brothers when he saw me. "Here's Izzie. Hey, Izzie, wanna see Eddie's new specimens?"

It took Eddie all of two seconds to switch sides. His scowl turned to a grin, and he stepped aside so I could look into his lab. Hanging from a short clothesline by their tails were three dead rats.

I screamed.

The boys hooted.

"What's all the commotion?" It was my mom, coming down the basement stairs, smiling.

Eddie slammed the door to his lab shut. He knew better than to get his brothers into trouble.

"Hi, Aunt Ana," Arturo said. His brothers echoed him.

"What's the joke?" she asked, and kissed them all.

"You don't want to know," Marita said.

"Probably not," Mom agreed. "Well, I just came down to say hi."

"Hi," my cousins all said again.

After my mom had climbed back up the basement stairs, I said, "What you did was really mean."

"Hey, he studies rat amino acids, right? We were just *helping*."

Even though some of Eddie's experiments sounded disgusting, at least he got his supplies, like the amino acid samples, from a lab supply catalogue. He didn't extract them from fresh rats.

"You could get diseases," I said. "How did you get them here?"

"Like this." Manny grabbed one of the rats off the line, and tossed it at me.

Marita and I both screamed.

The rubber rat bounced off my hip and fell to the floor.

Marita said, "You guys are really hilarious. Very, very funny."

When I recovered, I kicked the rubber rat away from me. "Come on, Marita. Let's go to your room."

Upstairs Marita shook a bottle of nail polish and untwisted the cap, pulled out the little brush, and carefully began brushing on the polish. When had she grown her nails?

"Put on a CD," she said, "I can't use my fingers for a few minutes."

I put on the one we had listened to all spring.

"Ugh! Not that one!" she said. "It's so tired."

"Then what?" I asked.

"See that red one? Sasha lent it to me. It is totally cool."

She blew gently on her nails.

As I put on the CD, I noticed my own hands. They were dry, and my nails were ragged from all the yard work. When I sat back down on the bed, I put my hands in my pockets.

"Hey, cuz, do you think there are cougars living in Oakland?"

Marita waved her hand to dry her nails and said, "No way! Have you ever seen a cougar in Oakland?"

"I mean in the hills, like in Redwood Park."

"As if," Marita said. As she began to paint the nails on her other hand, she sang softly with the CD. I hadn't even heard of this singer before, but Marita knew all the words.

"My acting class is going to do this big production at the end of the summer," Marita said, "and I am going to try out for—"

"Just a minute," I said, "I'll be right back."

Eddie was in his lab. I asked him his opinion about the cougars.

"Why exactly do you think there are cougars living in the hills? Is there any evidence?" He adjusted his glasses and seemed much more interested than Marita had been.

I told him about the meeting with James O'Donnell from the Department of Fish and Game.

Eddie listened carefully and then said, "Well, there's only one way to find out if there are any cougars living up there, and that's to do a thorough search."

"How would we do that?"

"Look for tracks." He jumped off his lab stool, as if he were headed for the hills that very moment.

"*Now?*" I asked.

"No, I'm going to find a map."

"I'll be up in Marita's room."

While waiting for Eddie, I told Marita, "You should see Charles, the boy who lives at the house where I work. He's really cute."

"Do you get to swim in their pool?" she asked.

I tried to toss my hair and laugh like Sylvia. "Of course not."

"Because you're their gardener."

Now she sounded like Sam.

"Charles would let me swim, if I wanted. I'd rather keep making my ten dollars an hour. I can swim any time."

The CD finished and the room felt too quiet.

"Want me to do your nails?" Marita asked.

Polish would look stupid on my dry and cracked nails. "No."

"Whatever," she said, turning to examine her skin in the mirror.

Marita was a year older than me, but it had never made a difference before. But next to her new CD and her acting and voice lessons, MEW seemed like a little kid's game. Like a lemonade stand, after all.

"Acting class is *so* fun," she said, suddenly switching to her new bubbly voice. "The other girls are so cool. Especially Sasha. We're going to be really close—probably best friends."

"But *I'm* your best friend."

"Oh, I know," Marita said, turning her back to me again. This time she examined her eyelashes in the mirror. "But you're my cousin. I mean, like, best friend outside of the family."

"Oh. Yeah. I know what you mean."

But I didn't.

Luckily Eddie came into Marita's room just then, clutching some maps.

"Okay, show me exactly where the Grays live," he said.

It took a while to find the right map, but once we did, it was easy to find Redwood Park. I used my finger to follow the route, from our neighborhood to Skyline Boulevard. Eddie used a magic marker to draw a circle around the spot where the Grays lived. "So," he said, "the cougar is suspected to be living in this vicinity." He waved the marker over the part of Redwood Park that was behind the Grays' house.

"Well, it hasn't been *seen*. That's the point. It may or may not exist."

"Okay, so where exactly did the kid say he was chased?"

I found the north ridge fire trail. "It would have been right about here."

"Good. So if we were to go look, we'd need to find an alternative entrance to the park. We can't go traipsing through your boss's yard. Ah! Here! We could get in the park right on the other side of the canyon behind the Grays' house. See here?"

While he concentrated on the map, Marita called someone. She spoke softly into the receiver, then giggled hysterically. I wondered who she was talking to.

"When do you want to go?" Eddie asked. "Tomorrow?"

"I have to work tomorrow," I said. "Maybe on Tuesday."

"Okay," Eddie agreed. "Tuesday."

"Hey, Marita!" I called out loudly, trying to inter-rupt her phone conversation. "Are you coming with us on Tuesday?"

Completely ignoring me, she shrieked at some-thing her friend said. She didn't get off the phone until supper was ready.

Before Mom and I left that night, I said to Marita, "We should go to the mall sometime. I have *tons* of money from my job. I want to buy some stuff."

eight

On Monday I called James O'Donnell at the Department of Fish and Game. "My name is Isabel Ramirez. I attended the cougar meeting on Skyline Boulevard a week ago."

"Yes, Isabel. How are you?"

"I'm fine. I was wondering what you decided about the depredation permit."

He spoke cautiously. "Actually, I'm writing up my report right now. I'll mail a copy to the Grays tomorrow."

"Are you issuing the permit?"

He paused. "Well, no, I'm not. My department hasn't been able to find any evidence of a mountain lion in Redwood Park. None whatsoever." He waited, as if he expected me to argue with him. When I didn't, he continued, "Now, south of the bay, as well as in the hills east of here, there is no doubt. We *know* there are some mountain lions living in those hills. They've been sighted. And their tracks, not to mention deer kills, are found frequently enough. But in the Oakland hills? Frankly, the young boy's story was very sketchy. Not a one of your neighbors has actually *seen* a mountain lion. It's possible that one wandered into the area briefly. But unlikely. We've researched the question thoroughly. So there will be no depredation permit, simply because there isn't a mountain lion."

I hung up, feeling both relieved and disappointed. I didn't want anyone killing a cougar, and yet I had liked thinking that something so wild lived right here in Oakland.

I called Eddie and told him the news. "So the search in Redwood Park tomorrow is off."

"Want to go to the pool instead?" Eddie asked.

"Okay. Is Marita coming?"

"She'll probably go with Sasha."

A picture of pretty Marita, giggling beside the pool with her aspiring actress friend, sprung to mind.

"I'm not sure," I said. "I think I have to work."

On Friday I returned to the Grays'. Sylvia answered the door in big orange sunglasses, an orange bikini, the telephone cradled between her ear and shoulder. She cupped her hand over the phone and told me, "Start by watering the potted plants and roses by the pool. Thanks, Isabel."

As I walked through the house to the patio door, I imagined *myself* in an orange bikini, stepping gracefully around the towels spread out at the public pool.

"What do you mean you won't be home tonight?" Sylvia's voice trailed after me. "You mean you'll be *late* or not home at *all*?" The phone slammed down, and her sandals flopped in my direction.

When I opened the patio door, Charles was climbing onto the diving board. Sylvia put a hand on my shoulder and quietly said, "Shh."

Charles stood on the end of the diving board, his back to the pool, his eyes closed. He took a deep breath, swung up his arms, and sprung off the board. For a moment his entire body splayed open, his back arched, head back, arms victoriously above his head. Then he tucked into a tight ball and only his hair flew wildly about his head. He made one, then two, somersaults in the air, straightening out again only at the last second, just as his arms hit the water.

It was perfect.

Sylvia pushed past me, clapping vigorously. "Bravo, Charles! That was *marvelous*."

She stood on the patio and watched while he climbed the diving board ladder again. This time he clomped to the end of the board as if he were wearing work boots. With arms and legs akimbo, he hurtled himself off the side of the board and did a loud belly flop. Pool water sprayed in all directions.

"Fine," Sylvia said, "throw away your talent." She went back in the house.

Charles hoisted himself out of the pool, noticed me, and said grumpily, "Hey, Isabel."

"Hi," I answered, and began uncoiling the hose. "That first dive was great. I'd give it a ten."

"I don't compete anymore."

"Why not?"

"It's too much work."

"The practicing?"

He just shrugged.

"But it must be really cool to be so good at something."

"Not really," he said. "*She* wants me to be good at it. *I* don't care."

A loud yelp interrupted our conversation. Sam hurdled over the back fence, ran to the pool, and jumped right in, still wearing his shorts and T-shirt. When he surfaced, shaking his curls and grinning, he said, "Scared you both!"

"As if," I said.

"I bet you haven't heard about the Department of Fish and Game's report!"

I played dumb and kept watering the roses.

"Mr. Bird Face says there is no cougar," Sam announced, using Charles's towel to dry his hair. "And if they don't think there's a cougar, then they won't miss one when it's gone."

I still ignored him. Charles, who was busy doing stretches, ignored him, too.

"You're just jealous because you're wasting your time doing dishes and pulling weeds. A real entrepreneur knows how to make big bucks fast."

"Ah, come on, Sam," Charles said. "The man said there was no cougar. That's their job. They know what they're talking about."

"Are you kidding? You're not using your head, Charles. Of *course* he's going to say there's no cougar. This way Mr. Big Beak gets to kill the cat himself and collect the ten thousand dollars for the gallbladder. Besides, how many times do I have to tell you I've seen the cougars?"

"It's a felony to kill a mountain lion," I told him.

"Thanks for the information, Easy Bell," Sam said. "Like I'm scared."

"Where would you get a gun, anyway?" I asked.

"That's easy. My father has a hunting rifle."

"Shut up, Sam," Charles said, tilting to the side as he stretched his leg muscles. "You're not going to hunt any cougar."

"Want to make a bet?" Sam challenged. *Some-one needs to protect this neighborhood.*"

"There's no cougar," I told him.

"What do you know, Easy Bell? Or is it Taco Bell?" Sam held his stomach and pretended to be dying laughing.

I swung around, the hose in my hand, and put my thumb across the nozzle ready to spray him. "Watch your mouth," I said. "I have a mess of cousins."

"Ooooooh, I'm scared," he mocked. He pretended to slick back his hair and gun low-rider engines.

"You should be," I threatened, spraying the ground around the roses so hard I made big holes in the soil.

"Chill out, Sam," Charles said.

"'A mess of cousins,'" Sam quoted, still guffawing. He jumped back into the pool.

"Don't listen to Sam," Charles said softly. "He doesn't mean anything. He's just a crazy guy."

I was mad, real mad, so I said, "He's a jerk and you're a loser."

Charles looked as if I had punched him in the stomach. My mouth again. I didn't know how to take it back, so I kept watering.

Charles was quiet the rest of the afternoon, but Sam never shut up, chattering about how he was going to spend the money he got from the cougar gallbladder. Before he left, the two boys made plans to go to the movies Saturday night.

"I'll come by at seven," Sam told Charles. Then to me he said, "Hey, Taco Bell, you tell your cousins I'm ready any time they are."

NINE

Saturday afternoon, when Mom and I arrived at
Aunt Lupe and Uncle Ed's, Arturo was all excited.
He had bought a car to take to college in the fall.

"A dark gold Duster," Aunt Lupe told us proudly.
"It's old, but in good condition. Hardly any scratches
or dents. The engine purrs."

"A real beaut," Uncle Ed agreed.

"When do we get to see it?" I asked. Arturo had
covered it with a tarp for protection.

"Now," Uncle Ed said. "Ready, Artie?"

All of us went around to the front of the house.
We stood in a half-circle on the sidewalk while
Arturo took a corner of the tarp between his thumb
and index finger. He looked at each of us, one by
one, then asked, "Ready?" He yanked the tarp off his
Duster with one sweep of his arm. To me, it looked

like a regular old used car. Big dark gold body. Black tires. Then I saw the windshield.

Everyone in the family gasped at once. The windshield was shattered, as if someone had taken a sledgehammer to it.

Arturo swore. Aunt Lupe didn't even tell him to watch his mouth. He'd only had the car for two days!

Arturo walked slowly toward the windshield and gently touched one of the spider cracks. Suddenly he whirled around and shouted, "I'll get you, you little—"

His brothers took off running, with Arturo chasing them. We all watched, confused. Then I walked over to the car and scraped at a corner of the windshield. A clear film—on which the image of shattered glass had been printed—began to peel away.

The adults cracked up. But Aunt Lupe said that the boys had gone too far again.

Good! The boys were in the mood for going too far—that meant it would be easy to talk them into my plan.

After we ate, I gathered my cousins in the basement. Marita flopped down on the couch, twisting her hair and looking bored. Until I started talking. Then even she got interested. I explained how Sam Spencer had been taunting me and that I didn't want to have to quit my job because of him. "So here's my idea. . . ."

My cousins loved the plan.

First, Arturo told the adults that we were going to take a ride in his new car. We'd be back in a couple of hours.

"A couple of hours? Where're you going?" Uncle Ed asked.

"Just up into the hills. A short demonstration drive. Then to get something to eat."

"We just ate!" Aunt Lupe cried.

"That was an hour ago," Tomas said. "By the time we drive around for a while, we'll be hungry again."

"They're old enough to drive around a bit, for goodness sake," Aunt Inez told Aunt Lupe. "We were much younger when we used to—"

"Never *mind*, Inez," Lupe said to her oldest sister.

Aunt Inez raised an eyebrow at my mom, who tried to look neutral.

"Okay," Aunt Lupe said, still scowling, "But not the girls."

"Why not?" asked Aunt Inez.

Aunt Lupe looked at Uncle Ed. Uncle Ed looked at Arturo.

Arturo said, "I'll take care of the girls."

"As if," I said.

"As if," Marita agreed.

The boys took more than an hour getting dressed, and I worried we'd be late. They each put on crisp white T-shirts, which was easy because Aunt Lupe was always buying them fresh under-wear. The older boys had baggy black pants, and Manny found a couple of gold chains in Aunt Lupe's jewelry box, which he and Arturo tried on.

"Take them off! You look like *muchachas!*" Tomas said in his best Spanglish imitation. He was busy drawing a rose, along with our area code, on his forearm.

"Anyone can see that's a ballpoint pen drawing, not a tattoo!" Marita said.

"We have to shave our heads," Manny declared, as if he were going to take a razor to his right now.

"You don't have time!" I said. "Let's go. Anyway, Sam isn't going to know the difference between real gang members and fake ones."

So Tomas and Manny pulled on beanies, while Eddie and Arturo greased back their hair with Vase-line. Then all six of us piled into the Duster, Manny and Tomas in the front with Arturo driving.

"This isn't going to work with Eddie and the girls in the backseat," Manny warned.

"You three are going to have to duck down when we get close," Arturo said.

"Not me!" Eddie protested.

"*Sí hermano chico,*" I said, getting in on the act. He was barely tall enough to see over the windowsill. With his big plastic glasses and pudgy cheeks, he would ruin our whole image.

'I'm older than you," he said to me, now getting truly angry, "don't call me little brother."

"You may be older," Marita put in, "but you're still littler."

"Okay, okay, Eddie," Arturo said. "But you have to take off your glasses."

"Then I won't be able to see anything!"

"Eddie," Marita explained. "The point is to scare this guy. You're about as scary looking as a cocker spaniel."

"You think taking off his glasses is going to turn him into a Doberman pinscher?" Tomas asked.

Eddie wasn't the only problem. Arturo drove as slowly as a grandma, with both hands gripping the steering wheel, at the ten o'clock and two o'clock positions. Even with the white T-shirt and greased hair, he looked a lot more like a college kid than a gang member.

In fact, all of my cousins looked pretty silly. Tomas rolled down the window so that he could prop his arm, with the ballpoint tattoo, on the sill. Arturo had found a couple of pairs of narrow black plastic sunglasses, which he and Tomas wore.

"Even Hollywood could do a better job creating a Chicano gang image," Marita observed.

"¡Silencio, chica!" Manny said.

"Ha!" Marita said, apparently forgetting her new girly personality. "No boy is going to silence me!"

But when we finally parked across from the Grays' house, all my cousins quieted down. Arturo said, "Okay, Izzie, tell us again what this clown looks like."

I described his curly brown hair and pug face. "He should be showing up about seven."

"It's five till," Eddie informed us, very seriously.

"You girls get down," Manny said as if we were doing a top-secret government job.

"Why me?" Marita asked, leaning over the front seat. "He doesn't know what I look like."

"Because girls aren't scary," Eddie answered. "Get down."

"Oh, like you're scary," she said.

"Like *any* of you are scary," I said.

"As if," Marita and I said at the same time.

"Fine," Tomas said angrily. "Then let's just leave."

"No, no, no!" I said. "I'm sorry. You're all very scary. *Very* scary."

Marita and I giggled.

"They're laughing at us," Manny said to his two older brothers.

Arturo smiled. "They *should* laugh. We don't even look like *stereotypes* of scary guys."

"Sam won't know the difference," I said.

"I hope not," Arturo answered, "because there he is." He started the engine. "Curly brown hair, right? Flat nose. That's our man."

Eddie cupped a hand over his mouth as if he were speaking into a walkie-talkie. "Young white male, approximately fourteen years old, wearing khakis and a blue T-shirt, walking suspiciously up street."

I started to rise up to have a look, but Eddie put a hand on my head and pushed me back down. "What's suspicious about him?" I asked, alarmed.

"Shh!" Tomas said.

Suddenly I had second thoughts about what we were doing. Sam had bragged about his father's rifle. What if he really took it?

Arturo gunned the engine of his Duster and started rolling down the street.

"What's he doing?" Marita hissed.

"Just walking," Eddie said. "We're following him now."

"I figure we'll just follow slowly for a while," Arturo said. "Get him warmed up."

"That's good," Marita laughed.

"We're easing up next to him now," Eddie reported. He rolled down his window.

Marita and I crouched closer to the floor of the backseat.

"Hey," Arturo said out his window.

Tomas snickered.

"What's he doing?" I whispered.

Eddie said, "He's speeding up. Pretending he didn't hear Arturo."

"Keep your voices down," Manny hissed.

"Hey, *chico*. Didn't you hear me talking to you?" Arturo was rolling the Duster along at the same pace Sam walked.

Sam said, "What do you want?"

He must have stopped walking because Arturo stopped the car. He said, "Do you know a girl named *Isabel*?" He pronounced my name the Spanish way.

"*Giiiiiirrrrrrl,*" Marita whispered to me.

Sam didn't answer. I would have given anything to see the look on his face.

"Yeah," Arturo continued in his Spanglish accent. "My homies and I have reason to believe that you do know *Isabel*. She's our cousin. We heard you are not as polite to her as you should be. Eh, *chico*?"

"Hey, she's a cool kid," I heard Sam say, his voice wavering and unnaturally high. He cleared his throat. "I just tease her sometimes."

"We suggest you treat her with respect." This was Tomas getting in on the act. "If not . . ." Tomas used his forefinger to tap the ballpoint area code on his arm. ". . . we got a lot more homies than you see in this jalopy."

"Oh, man, Tomas, you sound like a total dork," Manny hissed, sinking down in his seat.

"Our moms would *kill* us if they knew what we were doing," Marita whispered.

"Shh." I didn't want to miss a single world.

"Next time we follow you all the way home, *Sam Spencer.*" Arturo pushed his foot down on the accelerator. We shot down the street for several blocks, until Arturo turned a corner and pulled over. Marita and I jumped up off the floor and onto the seat next to Eddie.

"Whew," Arturo said, wiping sweat from his neck. "Well, Izzie." He turned around to look at me. "Do you think that'll do it?"

Then we all laughed so hard we had to open the car doors and fall out onto the sidewalk and street. We laughed so hard someone came out on her porch to see what the noise was all about.

"Let's get out of here," Tomas said. "Before someone thinks we're real trouble and calls *la policía.*"

Arturo drove us to Foster's Freeze and ordered french fries and Cokes. We sat at the picnic table in front of the drive-in because Arturo wouldn't let us eat in his car.

Tomas deepened his voice and imitated Arturo, "'My homies and I have reason to believe that you do know *Isabel.*'"

"Shut up," Arturo said. He filled his straw with Coke and sprayed Tomas.

"Hey, homeboy!" Tomas yelled.

"'We suggest you treat her with respect.'" This time it was Eddie, big glasses and high voice, imitating Tomas.

Marita and I laughed so hard, we both choked on the french fries we were eating.

"Laugh all you want," Manny said, not finding any of this funny. "But that guy was terrified. He won't bother you again."

"Yeah, and if he does, you know who to come to," Tomas added.

Arturo looked at his younger brothers and shook his head.

"What?" I asked him. "You don't think Sam was scared?"

Arturo held a hand out flat and rocked it, meaning, *maybe, maybe not.*

"Are you kidding?" Eddie shouted. "He was shaking in his boots! He could barely speak, he was so freaked."

"You won't have any trouble from him again," Tomas assured me.

"I'll let you know," I told him. "I have to go back there on Monday."

"Giiiiiiirrrrrrl," Marita said.

ten

I was glad I didn't see Charles or Sam that Monday. In fact, when they were not around on Wednesday or Friday either, I began to wonder if my cousins really had scared Sam. I liked that idea.

On Friday, after I finished my work, I climbed the ladder propped up behind the garden shed, reminding myself that there was nothing in this forest but big trees, and trees couldn't hurt me. Still, the way the bright sun poured through the branches, making a lace of light on the forest floor, reminded me of Hansel and Gretel, and everyone knows what happened to *them*. I forced myself to begin walking down the trail that led into the canyon. The splashing creek, the tangle of trees, the bushy squirrels. It was all so *wild* feeling.

After reaching the bottom, I crossed the creek and climbed the hill on the other side to the redwood grove. The blue tattered tent was still there.

"What are you doing here?" Sam was standing on the other side of the tent, a scoop of birdseed in his hand.

"This is *your* tent?" No wonder he sometimes came over the back fence into the Grays' yard.

"Yep." He emptied the birdseed into the feeder that hung from the tree behind the tent. Three jays swooped in for the fresh food, squawking and beating their wings at one another.

"Take turns," Sam told the jays. "There's enough for all of you guys."

Sam wouldn't meet my eyes. Maybe my cousins had actually scared him.

"What's the tent for?" I asked.

"I'm staking out the cougar."

"There is no cougar," I told Sam for about the tenth time.

Sam shrugged. "Believe what you want," he said. "I've seen them. They drink from the pool."

I knew he hadn't seen a cougar, and he definitely hadn't seen "them," as in more than one. My books and James O'Donnell all said cougars are loners. They stake out huge territories. The idea of a cougar drinking from the Grays' swimming pool was especially ridiculous.

For once I didn't argue with Sam. I felt kind of sorry for him, having to make up stories like that. He had crouched down and was tossing a peanut toward a squirrel. The squirrel scampered to the peanut, tucked it in its cheek, and hurried off with it. After storing the nut somewhere, the squirrel was back for another. This time it scampered right up to his hand.

"I've gotten a wren to perch on my finger," he said.

Sure, I thought. *And you've ridden bareback on a unicorn.* Out loud, I said, "I better get going."

"You don't believe me about the cougars."

"If you've seen a cougar, why didn't you say so at the meeting?"

"I *have* seen them," he said again. Then, knowing I didn't believe him, he added, "The proof is going to be one dead cat."

The way he talked, Sam made me think of what my books said about adolescent cougars, that they were the most likely to stray into places where they might get hurt.

"Dawn on Monday morning," he said. "When there are no people in the park. That's when the hunt is scheduled."

I knew a lot about older boys from my cousins. Sometimes they exaggerated themselves. But my cousins weren't as stupid as Sam. They didn't make up wild animals or imagine themselves fearless hunters.

I walked back down to the bottom of the canyon. When I reached the creek, I sat on a grassy spot for a moment and watched the creek water dance by. There was a jumble of rocks in the center of the creek where the water splashed up and caught the sunlight. Little strips of mud beaches on either side of the creek showed how high the water had been earlier in the spring.

A silly little newt, brown on its back and orange on its belly, scampered across the mud. Its four legs, each with five tiny fingers, shot straight out to the sides of its body. The newt made a pattern across the smooth mud. Newt tracks!

I stood up, realizing I'd better go home. As I was about to jump across the creek, I saw the other tracks.

Giant paw prints in the fresh mud. Cat paws. The largest cat paws I had ever seen in my life. This was no house cat. This wasn't even a bobcat. The tracks were enormous.

But how could that be? There were no cougars in Redwood Park. The Department of Fish and Game had said so.

Yet these tracks were not only mountain lion size, they were fresh. As if the big cat had taken a drink from the creek this very morning, then leapt to the other side and continued on its way.

I backed up slowly, trying to remember everything I had read about cougar encounters. Move slowly. Throw things. Don't run. I had to get out of this forest!

I tried to calm myself with the facts. I had about a thousand times better chance of getting killed in a car accident than by a cougar. The cat would be a lot more scared of me than I was of it. People kill a lot more cougars than the other way around.

Still. The way cougars attack from behind was pretty terrifying. They jump on their prey, knocking it to the ground. Then they bite into the back of the neck, killing instantly.

Stop thinking about it!

But I couldn't. Once the cougar has killed its prey, it uses a sharp claw just like a knife to rip open the side of the animal. First it drags out the guts and tosses these aside. Then the cougar eats its favorite parts, the liver and heart. Finally it buries the carcass for later meals.

Forcing myself to move slowly was torturous. Yet, if the cougar were lurking nearby, running could trigger a chase. Even though I was walking slowly, my breath came out as ragged and fast as if I were sprinting. I thought I would never reach the top of the canyon.

I was about two-thirds of the way there when the undergrowth ahead of me quivered. I stopped. It quivered again, as if it were coming to life.

Don't move, I told myself. *Look as big as possible.* I picked up a large stick and held it in front of me. I was hardly breathing. The undergrowth was still again.

Then a burst of movement. The branches shook hard. A big animal leapt onto the trail ahead of me.

A deer. A young deer with the beginnings of fuzz-covered antlers. It looked at me, panicked, then bounded up the hill, its hooves kicking holes in the soil.

It took me another five shaky minutes to reach the Grays' back fence. I threw myself up and over, into their yard in one fast movement. Then I leaned against the garden shed and tried to calm down.

Sam had been right. James O'Donnell had been wrong.

A cougar lived in Redwood Park.

Recently it had been here in this very canyon.

Sam said he had seen it—no, he said he had

seen *them*—drink from the pool. Could that be true?

When I came around to the other side of the garden shed, everything looked completely different. Too bright. Too sharp. All edges. The pool water glared and the hot flagstones burned.

eleven

As soon as I got home, I called the Department of Fish and Game, but they were closed for the weekend. Then the awful truth dawned on me. Sam hadn't spoken up at the cougar meeting because he wanted the cat to himself. He really *was* going to kill it and sell the gallbladder.

I turned on the TV, tried every station, and turned it off again. I opened the fridge about ten times, searched for something to eat, but I wasn't really hungry. I flipped through some of my cougar books, but I already had read them. Besides, they couldn't tell me what to do about a cougar living right here in Oakland, just a few miles up the hill. Or what to do about a boy who planned to kill the cougar on Monday morning. Most important of all, the books couldn't tell me if the cougar *should* be killed.

Finally, trying to make myself feel better, I pulled my money out from under my mattress. My mom kept telling me I had better put it in the bank, but I liked being able to see, hold, and count the cash. I laid it out on my bed now, piling up the twenties in one stack, the tens in another, and so on. I counted it, though I knew exactly how much was there. Two hundred and seventy-four dollars.

"So what," I said out loud. I mussed up the stacks of bills. "Big deal."

I scooped up the money, for once not making sure the stacks stayed neat, and shoved it under my mattress again. My entrepreneurial endeavor was a success, I had great cash flow, but so what?

I grabbed my suit and towel and ran the entire distance to the public pool. It was a gigantic rectangle, with black lines painted on the bottom to make racing lanes. The deck was all cement, surrounded by a tall chain-link fence with curls of barbed wire at the top. My cousins were all there, even the older boys. Marita was lying on a towel next to another girl. Forgetting all about trying to imitate tall and elegant Sylvia Gray, I walked slowly toward them, wishing I were a foot shorter, wishing I had at least tied back my wild hair and reminding myself not to smile.

"Cuz!" Marita said, jumping to her feet. She

scooted her towel over, making a space between her and the other girl. "Put your towel here."

I accidentally smiled. Then covered my mouth with my hand.

"This is my cousin Izzie," Marita said. "This is Sasha."

I was surprised to see that Sasha had short black hair and was sort of chubby. She said, "Marita always talks about you."

"She does?"

Sasha nodded. As I laid out my towel, she reached over to touch my hair. "You have the *coolest* hair. I wish my hair did something other than just sit flat on my head."

I stretched out, feeling the warmth of the sun. Across the pool Arturo jackknifed off the diving board. Then Eddie did a corkscrew jump, holding his nose. Tomas and Manny were talking to the lifeguard, a tanned blonde who looked like she was ignoring them. I laughed out loud.

"What's so funny?" Marita asked.

"I don't know. I guess I'm just happy to be here."

"It's about time you *got* here. Geez, a whole month of summer is practically over."

Just then it occurred to me that, even though I thought Marita had deserted me for a new best friend, maybe I deserted *her*. After all, I was the one who had quit coming to the pool and hadn't had time to hang out at the mall.

I kicked her gently. "Thanks for helping Saturday night."

Marita sat up. "That was so fun. Did it work? Has he been bothering you?"

We told Sasha, in great detail, how my cousins had posed as gang members to scare Sam Spencer.

"He must be a real jerk," Sasha said.

"Sort of," I said. When he called me Easy Bell, or worse, and made fun of me, I hated him. But now I felt confused. He hadn't been lying about the cougar after all. Remembering how terrified I had felt this morning, after seeing the tracks, I wondered if maybe he was also right that it needed to be killed. I didn't like the idea of a cougar crushing my skull. Devouring my heart. Burying my body for later gorging. I didn't like being prey.

I changed the subject, and Marita, Sasha and I talked about music and our families for the rest of the day. Sasha was really nice, and we had so much fun we never even went in the water.

In the late afternoon Sasha's mom picked her up, and my cousins and I walked home together. A cool breeze blew in off the bay. Arturo bought ice cream for all of us at Foster's Freeze. As he handed out the cones, it seemed like he wasn't even one of the kids anymore. In two months he would be living in a dorm at the university.

We walked slowly, eating ice cream and taking up the whole sidewalk. I wished I could do this tomorrow, and the next day, and the day after that. I wished I had never met Sam Spencer. I wished I had never seen the cougar tracks.

"Hey, Izzie," Arturo said quietly, dropping back to talk to me. "How're you doing?"

"Fine."

"Is that kid still bothering you?"

"Not really." At least not in the same way.

"How's the entrepreneurial endeavor going? Making big bucks?"

"Yeah."

"Good. I'll be able to count on you if I get in some kind of financial jam at school next year, right?"

He was kidding, but I wasn't when I said, "Always."

Arturo put an arm around my shoulders. "Seriously, Izzie. You'll let me know if you need help with anything, all right?"

I nodded and looked away because I didn't want him to see how upset I felt.

After my cousins dropped me off at my house, I went straight over to Aunt Inez's, walking smack into another poker game. Three jovial women, plus Aunt Inez, sat with fans of cards in their hands, shouting jokes.

"Hi, Aunt Inez," I said, putting one hand on her shoulder and reaching over with the other to scoop some guacamole onto a tortilla chip.

"It's the party food mooch!" said one of her friends.

"Isn't this the one who started her own gardening business?" asked another.

"Yard work," I corrected.

"How's it going, honey?"

"Fine, thanks," I muttered. "Aunt Inez, can I talk to you for a minute?"

"Wait, I have a great hand."

"Aunt Inez, you're not supposed to *tell* them."

"Inez couldn't bluff if her life depended on it," one of her friends said.

"What's wrong with having an honest face?" she asked.

"Nothing, unless you're trying to win at poker."

Hah. Hah. Hah.

"Aunt Inez, please?" I pulled at her arm.

She got up and we went into the room off her kitchen, where she sat on an oversized bag of kitty kibble and looked at me more carefully. "Izzie, are you all right?"

I had planned on telling Aunt Inez everything. About Charles's ruined diving career, about Sam's taunting, about the cougar meeting and James O'Donnell from the Department of Fish and Game, about the cougar tracks in the mud. But instead, I said, "I'm fine. Maybe I'll come back another time when you don't have company."

Bursts of laughter came from the front room, but Aunt Inez didn't even blink in that direction. She put her hands on my shoulders. "Izzie, I think you had better tell me what's wrong. It's something about your job, isn't it?"

"I think I can handle it, Aunt Inez."

"Inez!" someone shouted from the front room. "Are you in this hand or not?"

"You better get back in the game. I'm fine!" I jumped up and darted through the room of poker players.

"How's school going, Izzie?" someone asked.

"It's summer, you idiot!" another lady answered.

Hah. Hah. Hah. Hah. Hah. Hah.

I grabbed a handful of chips and slipped out the front door.

That night Mom and I watched a couple of dumb shows on TV. I didn't even know I had fallen asleep until I woke up sometime in the middle of the night. Mom had left me on the couch, covered with a blanket. As I crawled up the stairs to my bed, I remembered the dream I had just had.

I was swimming in the Grays' pool. A cougar—with its golden coat, gigantic paws, black and white muzzle, black-lined eyes, and black-tipped tail—paced around the pool while I swam. It paced and paced and paced, its stomach swaying back and forth, its head hung low, but its eyes watching me the whole time. I dog-paddled in the water, keeping my eyes on the big cat.

And yet—even though I couldn't get out of the pool because of the cougar, even though I had to keep swimming no matter how tired I was, even though the cougar circled, around and around, always watching me—it wasn't a scary dream. Rather than feeling terrified, as I had when I saw the tracks by the creek, I felt happy. I didn't feel trapped by the cougar; I felt guarded by it. We weren't exactly friends, but we were connected. It was as if we knew each other very well.

I knew then that I had to save the cougar. I had seen its tracks. I had dreamt about it. That cougar felt like a door to the rest of my life. Wild and free. Living where it wasn't supposed to live, at least according to some people. Hunting, roaming, exploring in the hills, right here in Oakland. Right here in *my* hometown. No matter how scary it was, I didn't want the cougar to die.

Much later that day, at the family barbecue, I found Arturo reading a textbook in his room.

"Studying *already?*"

"It's good to get a jump on things, Izzie."

"Remember yesterday when you said to ask if I needed help with anything?"

"Sure. What's up?"

"I need you to drive me somewhere at five o'clock Monday morning."

"Five o'clock?"

"Please keep your voice down. This has to be just between you and me."

"Izzie—"

"You said if I ever needed anything." Arturo had become too much of an adult this year. If I told him what I planned on doing, he might try to stop me. I added, "I'll find another way to get where I'm going if you don't take me. It would be better if you came along."

"I have tomorrow off. No way am I getting up at—"

"You said anything I needed."

Arturo sighed. "All right," he agreed reluctantly.

I held out my hand to shake. "But you have to promise to tell *no one*. Promise?"

Arturo ignored my hand and threw an arm around my neck. "I'll pick you up Monday morning. But the second you get in the car, I want the full story of where we're going and why. If I decide we're *not* going, then we're not. Deal?"

"Deal."

Next I found Eddie in his lab and told him I needed that map he had showed me the week before.

"The one that shows how to get into your cougar canyon?"

"Yeah."

"Why?"

"Never mind, Eddie. Could I please just have the map?"

He slammed down a beaker. "You're all secretive and stuck-up this summer." Eddie huffed off to his room and returned with the map.

I said, "Thank you," and he slammed the door to his lab shut behind him.

twelve

On Monday morning my alarm rang at four-thirty. I woke up with the same feeling I had had on the last day of school. As if my destiny were just under my skin.

I dressed quickly and tiptoed down to the kitchen, leaving a note saying Arturo and I were going up to Redwood Park to look for wildlife. It was the truth.

Then I quietly let myself out of the house. It was still dark, and I stayed on the porch until Arturo's gold Duster drew up in front. When I pulled open the passenger door, I was shocked that the front seat was already crowded with Eddie and Marita.

"I said just *you*," I barked at Arturo.

Marita had her arms crossed over her chest and her lips pressed together.

Eddie said, "Hurry up and get in the backseat before Aunt Ana wakes up."

Arturo took off. Eddie had a headlamp strapped on his forehead and was studying a map. "Get on the freeway," he said, then clicked off the headlamp.

"How do you know where we're going?" I asked Eddie. "Arturo, I *told* you not to bring anyone else."

"You think you're such a big shot this summer," Marita said, whirling around in her seat. "You think you can just leave me out of everything."

"No, I don't," I said weakly.

"We already know what you're doing, anyway," Eddie said. Then to Arturo, "Take the Skyline exit." Back to me, "You're going to look for the mountain lion. I didn't believe you when you said it didn't exist."

"Yeah, you just wanted to keep it to yourself. Like everything else this summer," Marita snapped.

Her accusations hurt. I hadn't meant to be secretive. I hadn't meant to leave her out. I leaned back in the car seat. Most of the houses we passed were still dark, their people still sleeping. The cougar, too, might be curled up in its den, sleeping. Just about to get up for its dawn prowl. I had to get to it before Sam did. I needed to concentrate on the cougar, not on Marita's anger.

Still, I couldn't help saying, "You said Sasha was your best friend now. You spend all your time with her."

"That's because you got a job and suddenly have all these secrets." She crossed her arms dramatically.

"Come on, you two," Arturo said. "Lighten up. Tell us your plan, Izzie. Why are we looking for the cougar, anyway?"

"I wasn't lying to you, Eddie," I said. "James O'Donnell, the man from the Department of Fish and Game, convinced me that there *wasn't* a cougar. But he's wrong. I saw tracks on Friday. So I know it's there. And—" This was the hard part. "I think Sam is going to try to kill it. Probably this morning at dawn. If we go into the canyon and make lots and lots of noise, the cougar will be warned."

"Wait a minute." Arturo swerved the car off the road and pulled the parking brake.

"Sam?" Eddie asked. "That kid we scared on Saturday night? He thinks he's going to kill a cougar?"

"More details, Izzie," Arturo demanded, turning around in the seat to look me in the eye.

"Sam wants to kill the cougar and sell its gallbladder. They go for up to ten thousand dollars. In some cultures bear gallbladders are thought to have healing powers. The cougar's gallbladder looks just like a bear's."

"You mean," Eddie said, "he's going to shoot the cougar and then carve out the gallbladder?"

"This is *so* gross," Marita said, clearly interested. She jumped onto her knees so she could face me in the backseat.

"No way," Arturo said. "How's that kid going to kill a cougar? Who does he think he is, Hercules or something?"

"He's going to use his father's hunting rifle," I said with growing impatience. "Come *on*. We're going to be too late if you don't drive now."

"How does he know where the cougar is?" Arturo continued to ask his slow, deliberate questions.

"He has a tent in Redwood Park. He's been staking it out."

"No," Arturo said suddenly. He started the car engine. "We're going home."

"Arturo, *yes*. You *have* to help me. The cougar is my destiny. You don't understand."

"You're right. I don't. I'm not taking my baby sister and baby brother and baby cousin into a dark forest where a crazy kid who calls you racist names is going to be shooting his daddy's rifle. You're right: There's nothing about this I understand."

"Then I'll walk up there." I got out of the back-seat and slammed the car door.

Marita rolled down her window and said, "You're *loca,* girl." But I could tell she was impressed.

"The fact of the matter is," Eddie said, "Izzie is right. By law, the cougar has a right to live in Red-wood Park. Sam Spencer is committing a felony by shooting the catamount. Izzie is actually correct in wanting to protect the puma."

Eddie was showing off that he knew all the different names for mountain lions. But that meant he had been reading about them. That he cared. That maybe he'd take my side.

"You're just afraid," I told Arturo.

That cougar was *mine.* I dreamed about her. I found her tracks. I was the only one who knew of Sam's plan. If I didn't save her, no one would.

Marita was silent, her eyes chasing from me to Arturo to Eddie and back to me. Then suddenly she said, "Sam Spencer called Izzie those names. He acted like she wasn't even supposed to be in his neighborhood. Izzie has a right to be in any neighbor-hood she wants. So do we. So does the cougar. The cougar's people were here before Sam's people."

"Cougars don't have people, Marita," Eddie corrected.

"You know what I mean."

Arturo glanced at his watch, took a couple of big heaving sighs. I saw him waver, so I said, "Arturo, I'm *thirteen* years old. I can make my own decisions. After all, I have my own successful entrepreneurial endeavor."

"Yeah!" Eddie and Marita said in unison. I had won the twins over.

"All right," Arturo sighed. "You might be thirteen, but I'm in charge. We'll drive up there, but no one makes a move once we're there unless I say so."

"So hurry," I said, jumping back in. "We'll be late."

We rode in the dark silence as the car climbed up into the hills. I watched the sky lighten, hoping that we would be on time. Eddie continued to read the map and give Arturo directions.

"It's good you two came," I said to the twins, trying to make up. "The more of us there are, the more noise we can make."

"Not to mention the fact that I've charted our exact route to the other side of that canyon," Eddie added. "Okay, Arturo when you reach the Lupine Campground, punch your odometer. It should be exactly three point eight miles beyond there. We can park at the Muir picnic area."

I watched the sky turn pink with morning. By now we were in the heart of Redwood Park, the winding road lined by huge evergreens. Rays of sun shot out above the trees to the east.

Arturo drove slowly. The minutes seemed like hours, but finally Eddie said, "Here! Pull over next to that pickup truck."

Arturo pulled in alongside the truck, his Duster facing the woods. We all sat in the car for a moment and looked into the trees. Though the sky was already light, the woods were still dark.

"What do you say I just honk my horn a lot," Arturo said. "Do you think that would be enough noise to warn the cougar?"

"It's a big canyon," I told him. "We have to go in there."

"No way," Arturo said.

"How do you know the cougar is in *this* canyon?" Eddie asked.

"I don't. But this is where I saw the tracks."

"The sun is rising," Arturo said. "Can't we just wait a few minutes more, until it's not so dark in there?"

My dream was still so clear to me. The cougar pacing around the pool. Me swimming. The two of us guarding each other. There was no time to waste. I opened my car door and got out. Marita did the same.

"You coming?" she asked, poking her head back into the car.

"Oh, man," Arturo said, getting out of the car slowly.

Marita hooked her arm in mine. "Let's go."

"In *there*?" Arturo balked.

"We have to," I said. "There's a trail. See? Here's the beginning of it. Eddie, you go first with your headlamp."

"I can't believe this," Arturo said, rubbing his forehead.

"What's not to believe? It's Izzie's destiny," Marita told him. I looked at her quickly, thinking she was making fun of me, but she wasn't. "And she's my best friend, so I'm helping. You gotta come, too, Eddie, because you're my twin. And Arturo, you're the oldest, so you have to, as well. Let's go."

Still holding my arm, Marita marched toward the trailhead. Apparently she had gotten over her bubbly personality stage. I followed her onto the trail.

"Wait!" Eddie called out. "Fresh dog scat!"

"Gross, Eddie!" Marita said. "Come *on*."

"It might be significant."

"It might mean," Arturo said, "that the guy in this blue pickup truck brought out his dog for an early morning run. Big deal."

"Dogs, plural," Eddie corrected. "There's enough fresh scat here for at least three dogs."

"Eddie's right," I said. "I'm taking down this truck's license number."

"Since when is walking your dogs in the morning illegal?" Arturo asked, still rubbing his forehead.

Suddenly I heard the sound of a dog barking, deep down in the canyon. Then another dog barked.

"They sound far away," Eddie said. "Why would someone take his dogs way down into a pitch dark canyon before daylight?"

"Let's go see," I suggested.

Marita and I went first. Eddie was right behind us, his headlamp making a weak beam of light on the trail. I stepped carefully, making sure my sneakers tread silently on the soil.

Eddie whispered, "I thought the plan was to make lots of noise."

"Shh," Marita whispered back to him. "Then the cougar will know where we are!"

"But that's the whole point," Eddie argued, still in a whisper. "We don't want to sneak up on the cougar. That would be the worst possible scenario."

"Don't start in on *scenarios*," Marita hissed.

Arturo followed the three of us silently. I think he was the most scared of all.

"Okay," Eddie said, trying to speak up. "We have to start making noise. Izzie's plan was a good one, to warn the cougar that people are around. Ready? On the count of three—"

Eddie never got to count to three. Suddenly a whole chorus of barking broke out, as if there were a pack of wild dogs in the canyon. I heard branches breaking, a man's shout, animals crashing through the undergrowth. The barking grew to a frenzy. The dogs sounded so wild and hungry that I could picture the saliva flying from their rubbery muzzles.

Marita squeezed my arm so tightly it hurt.

"Back to the car," Arturo ordered, but none of us moved. We all stood looking into the blackness of the forest, listening to the racket. I held my breath. Marita was still clamped onto my arm. Before I could even guess what had made the dogs so crazy . . .

A gunshot tore open the pink morning.

Then silence. A silence like no other silence I had ever heard. It was as if God took that gunshot by the throat, was about to strangle it, then let go.

A moment later the dogs began growling and snarling again. I took off, running toward them, making my way down the trail, stumbling in the hazy forest dawn. "Izzie!" Arturo shouted after me, "Izzie! Stop!"

Daybreak shot arrows of sunshine through the treetops, but they didn't quite reach the forest floor. Even so, my eyes adjusted and I followed my ears, heading for the dogs and men's voices. I heard the pounding of feet behind me.

"Izzie," Arturo tried to talk to me again. "He has a rifle. You can't just—"

I thought of that picture in the newspaper of the cougar, her mouth open, her tongue withdrawn, as if she were screaming. I thought of the cougar in my dream, how perfectly I understood her.

"There he is!" I cried.

Sam Spencer was charging up the trail toward us, probably trying to get to his blue tent as a hideaway. His face was twisted, as if he were in pain, and he barely even acknowledged my presence. "Move," he said, running by me on the trail.

"You won't get away with this," I screamed to his back. He headed up the trail toward the road.

"I didn't see a gun," Eddie said. "Or the gall-bladder."

"He probably already stashed them in the forest," I said.

"What should we do now?" Marita asked.

Eddie cupped a hand around his ear. "It sounds like the dogs are heading back up toward the truck, but by a different trail. I can hear them over in that direction."

"Sam's gunshot probably scared them out of their minds," I said.

Arturo looked over his shoulder. I could tell he wanted us all to just leave Redwood Park, but it didn't seem very safe in the direction of the car, where Sam had just run. Then he looked down into the canyon. "Let's go see," he said softly.

The four of us walked, slowly now, down the trail. We didn't speak. My feet felt like weights. It was as if time had stopped. Eventually, though, I could hear the music of the creek, still splashing toward the Pacific Ocean, as if nothing in the forest had changed.

Just as the creek came into view below us, I saw the great furry bulk lying on the ground under a tree. I knelt down beside the enormous cat. His muzzle was white and black, with whiskers nearly a foot long. The eyes were closed and blood spilled from a wound just in front of his big ear. I touched his shoulder, then lifted a huge paw. The pad was rough and scratchy from hours and hours of prowling his range.

"We're too late," I whispered. "The cougar is dead."

thirteen

The entire forest seemed to swirl in my vision. My cougar. The door to the rest of my life. My destiny. Dead. I had come too late. I hadn't been able to save him.

My cousins held back, but I stayed right by its side. Behind me I could hear Arturo getting down on his knees, like he was going to pray. Seeing an animal this beautiful, right here in Oakland, was like being able to see God for a moment. Seeing it *dead* tore open a big ragged place inside me.

I was startled by the sound of someone splashing across the creek. It was Charles, running right through the water and heading toward us. His blond hair was flying, and his face was wet with sweat, maybe even tears.

"Izzie," he panted, out of breath, unable to say more.

"Did you help him kill it?" I accused.

He just looked at me, his chest heaving, his arms hanging at his sides.

"You and Sam murdered the cougar," I yelled. "What are you doing back here now? Are you going to get the gallbladder?"

Charles shook his head. Still trying to catch his breath, he bent over and placed his hands on his knees. He lowered his head, and his sweat-wet hair hung down.

Arturo came up behind me and placed his hands on my shoulders. "Wait until he can talk," he said softly to me.

"They hired professional hunters," Charles finally blurted. "It's easy with dogs. The dogs chased the cougar up the tree. Then they shot it out of the tree."

So Sam had used his blue tent hideaway to study the cougar's habits. Then he'd told the hunters when and where they could find the cat. After he'd helped someone else kill it, he'd run away like a coward.

"Why?" I asked.

"People were scared," Charles said. "The cougar could have hurt someone."

"But the cougar *didn't* hurt anyone," I cried.

How stupid to kill something just because it frightens you. Even if it has claws the size of my fingers. Even if it has jaws stronger than steel traps. Even if it was wilder than the night sky.

"I know," Charles said, still breathing hard. He crouched down beside me and reached out a hand. Carefully, he touched the lion's coat, then petted it in the direction of the fur. "You should have seen it," he said so quietly it was as if he was speaking only to himself. "I saw him running, being chased by the dogs, right before he was shot. He was the most beautiful animal I've ever seen in my life. If a diver could be even *half* that graceful . . ." Charles didn't even try to wipe away the tears that wet his cheeks. I pet the big cat with him, my hand following his.

For a long time Charles and I sat by the lion. I touched his fuzzy ear, then his long, thick eyelashes.

A complete stillness finally caught my attention. Marita and Eddie were both gone. "Where did the twins go?"

"They ran back toward the car," Arturo said. "They must have gotten scared. We better go find them." Arturo gently tried to pull me to my feet, but I wouldn't budge.

"I'm staying."

"Izzie—" Arturo began in his sternest voice. He was interrupted by Marita bursting back down the trail, Eddie behind her.

"Got a good ID," Eddie announced. His big glasses had slid to the tip of his nose.

"The hunters were at the truck," Marita added.

"Do you have your notebook, Izzie?" Eddie said. "Write this down. Two men, both white, one six foot two inches, the other approximately five foot ten. Long brown hair in a ponytail on the tall guy, reddish crew cut on the other."

"That blue pickup belonged to the hunters?" I asked.

"Duh," Marita said. "Remember the, uh, doggie-do-do?"

"How come they hadn't already driven away?" I asked.

"When we got there, they were kicking the truck and cursing. They had two flat tires! They couldn't go anywhere." Eddie was so excited, he swallowed his words. "When they saw us, they took off running into the woods on the other side of the highway."

"What about Sam? Did you see him?" I asked.

Eddie and Marita both shook their heads.

Hiding. What a coward.

"As soon as they shot the cougar, I ran home to call Fish and Game," Charles said. "They aren't open yet, but I left a message for O'Donnell to come right away. I'll call again at eight."

That turned out to be unnecessary. James O'Donnell showed up just before eight.

Sunlight splashed down through the branches and brightened the forest floor. The cougar lay in a pool of light. He looked like a big wild angel to me, an angel with whiskers and a black nose.

"It's an adolescent male," O'Donnell said, crouching down and examining the cat. "Probably hasn't been in the canyon long. Probably still trying to find his own range."

Charles asked, "Are you going to prosecute the hunters?"

"Absolutely. To the full extent of the law. The actual hunters, as well as anyone involved in hiring them. It's a felony to shoot a cougar."

Eddie and Marita gave James O'Donnell the license number of the blue pickup truck and the descriptions of the men with the dogs and rifles. I wondered how much money the hunters were paid. Money for a dead cougar. How can you put a price tag on a life?

I thought of Sam sitting by the swimming pool,

earlier this summer, saying, *Ten thousand dollars, man. It'll be easy. We'll be rich.*

Then I thought of me smart-mouthing, *Money is power.*

Maybe Sam and I had made some of the same mistakes. Maybe that was why I didn't mention him to Mr. O'Donnell.

I knelt down next to the cougar for the last time. I petted its paw, its muzzle, some belly fur, then crawled over to touch the black tip of its tail. Destiny means the things that happen to you that you don't choose. Doom or fortune.

"I'm sorry," I told the cougar. "I'm really, really sorry."

fourteen

Having the cookout in Redwood Park, as a memorial to the cougar, was Aunt Inez's idea. But for a few weeks I refused. I felt awful that I hadn't been able to save the mountain lion. The hunters, as well as the men who had hired them, had been caught. Thanks to both of the twins for running back up the hill and getting good descriptions of the hunters. Thanks especially to the fact that the hunters had two flat tires and hadn't been able to escape fast enough.

All I had done was *try* to save the cougar. And failed.

Not only that, but Mom had also made me quit working at the Grays'.

But Aunt Inez was stubborn about her memorial cookout idea. She wouldn't give up. A few weeks after the cougar's death, at the end of July, she came over for dinner on a Wednesday.

"Hey, Izzie, I found this beautiful poem about mountain lions, written by—"

"No."

Aunt Inez and Mom exchanged looks. They always thought they were being so sly. The minute she mentioned mountain lions, Aunt Inez came over to talk me into the memorial cookout idea.

"I think it'll help," she said. "We can all say good-bye to the mountain lion together."

"No."

"Oh, Izzie, you can't sulk the rest of the summer," my mom said.

"You're not God," Aunt Inez said. "You're a thirteen-year-old human being."

"A thirteen-year-old human being who got in over her head," my mom added. Then I got the lecture again about not telling my mom everything. Lies of omission, she called them.

"Give her a break, Ana," Aunt Inez argued.

"Inez, do you mind if I do my own child-rearing?"

"Okay," I said suddenly, because I felt like taking Aunt Inez's side, not because I wanted to do the memorial cookout. "I'll do it."

As it turned out, Aunt Inez was right. Planning the memorial cookout helped. Even before the cookout, between Wednesday night and Saturday afternoon, I did a lot of thinking. I had a few questions about the cougar. And I knew who would have the answers.

On Saturday morning, after Mom left to finish putting in a lawn for a client, I rode up to the Grays' house. When no one answered the front door, I went around to the backyard.

Charles was midair, flying above the blue water. He seemed to hover there longer than was humanly possible, then splashed into the pool.

"Your feet!" boomed a deep voice. Until he spoke, I hadn't even noticed the tall man who stood on the other end of the pool. "Your feet were catty-wonk. Again. Mind your shoulders, too."

Charles hefted himself out of the pool and climbed the diving board rungs. I remembered his words. *He was the most beautiful animal I've ever seen in my life. If a diver could be even half that graceful . . .* Maybe Charles had seen the same thing I saw. The waste of that beauty.

I backed up quietly, before he could see me. I didn't think I should interrupt his diving lesson. I was leaving when I heard a hiss.

It clearly didn't come from Charles, who was underwater at that moment. But there was a figure in the shade by the garden shed.

Sam sat with his back against the fence, his hands behind his head. "It's Easy Bell," he said as I approached. "Or maybe it should be Tinker Bell, the way you keep showing up."

"You could just call me Izzie. It's easier."

"Izzier? Who could be Izzier than you?"

"Is that Charles's diving coach?"

Sam nodded.

"What are *you* doing?"

"Waiting for his lesson to end." He pulled his knees up to his chest. "I'm not supposed to be here. Sylvia would only pay for the lessons if he promised to work hard. The coach said neither she nor I were supposed to be around during the lesson."

"Is he diving again because of the cougar?"

"What would *that* have to do with it?" But the way Sam lowered his eyes and looked away from me, I could tell that he knew what I was talking about.

"Hey! You two! Out!" The coach clapped his hands like Sam and I were two stray dogs that had wandered into the yard.

"Hi, Izzie!" Charles called out.

"That's it, Charles. You tell your friends to leave, or else—"

Sam jumped to his feet. "I'm leaving," he yelled to the coach. Sam used the ladder to hop the fence.

I followed, calling after him, "Why did you help them kill the cougar?"

He turned abruptly. "I didn't."

"I saw you talking to the men who hired the hunters, that night after the meeting."

For once Sam didn't have a quick comeback. He thought for a moment, then said, "No one believed I'd seen the cougar. *You* didn't. Even Charles didn't. So I told *them*. And they believed me." Sam squatted and stirred the soil with a stick. He said, "It was a mistake."

"But you wanted to kill it yourself! You said you were going to sell the gallbladder and get rich!"

Sam shrugged. He looked longingly over his shoulder, as if he wanted to escape to his tent. I began remembering things—him feeding the squirrels and blue jays, the way he hadn't wanted to squash a daddy longlegs on the lounge chair, him cuddling Sylvia's dogs. That's when I realized something else: Sam was all talk.

I said, "*You're* the one who let the air out of the hunters' tires, aren't you? That's why you were running up the trail!"

Sam looked up sharply. "None of your business. Why are you always snooping?"

"I guess I'm curious."

"Mind your own business." But now he actually looked scared.

"That was brave," I said. "Whoever did it, I mean."

"Well, it wasn't me," he said. "If those men find out who did do it . . ."

"That person might be in a lot of trouble."

Sam nodded. "Once I knew they were really going to hunt the cougar with dogs, there was no way I could stop them. I tried to get there first, real early, and warn the cougar."

"That was my idea, too," I said.

"But I had to do it without being seen."

Now I understood everything. If Sam and Charles had been discovered trying to interfere with killing the cougar, their neighbors, the men who hired the hunters, would be angry.

"You know what I think? Even if you *hadn't* told those men about the cougar, they would have hunted it anyway. They were already convinced it existed."

Sam looked at me for a long moment. Then he actually smiled. Not smirked, *smiled*.

A moment later he had disappeared down the trail.

That afternoon all ten of us—Aunt Inez, Aunt Lupe, Uncle Ed, Arturo, Tomas, Manny, Eddie, Marita, Mom and I—drove up to the Muir picnic area, across the road from where my cousins and I had entered the forest on the morning the cougar was killed.

We brought charcoal, marinated chicken, potato salad, fruit salad, chips, sodas, and a big pan of flan that I made. Everyone brought flowers, too, and we covered two picnic tables with glass jars filled with irises, poppies, lavender, cosmos, verbena, whatever we found blooming in our gardens. I picked a bunch of lupine from along the roadside in Redwood Park, flowers from the cougar's own garden, and added those to the bouquets.

After we had barbecued the chicken, we crowded around one picnic table. Uncle Ed raised his soda to make the first toast. "In memory of the young mountain lion."

"To the safety of young creatures of all species," my mom said.

"To cats everywhere," Aunt Inez added.

"To Izzie's bravery," Arturo toasted.

"To all wild animals," Marita said. "Like my cousin Izzie."

Everyone laughed.

For them, it was all over. But I still had that uneasy feeling in my arms and legs. Seeing the wild forest, the cougar's death, even learning about Sam, those things had made my restlessness only worse.

After eating, Uncle Ed stretched out on top of an empty picnic table. He said it was good for his back, and then he fell right to sleep. My cousins started a poker game at another table, while my mom and aunts argued about something as they cleaned up.

I crossed the road and headed down the trail into the cougar's canyon. Once in the forest, I ran to the redwood grove. If Sam was in his tent, he didn't answer. He must have been there recently, though, because the blue jays were eagerly eating from the newly filled feeder. I continued down to the creek where I'd seen the cougar tracks.

Gravity pulls water downstream, deeper into the canyon, and that afternoon I felt gravity pulling me, too. I followed the creek, walking along its banks, crossing small meadows and climbing over tumbled piles of stones. The going was easy for a while, but soon thickets of willow closed in around the streambed. Still I pushed forward, shoving aside the high branches and stepping over the low ones.

Soon I was in the deepest part of the canyon, far from anyone's back fence. Marita had called me a wild animal in her toast, and I felt like one now, as if I were moving by instinct alone.

Finally the thick underbrush gave way to bays, alders, and a couple of big oaks. The creek widened, turned a corner, and then dropped into a small but steep ravine bordered by gray boulders. I hopped up on a big boulder and slid down the other side.

And there the creek water gathered in a basin of stones, forming a deep pool.

Sunlight poured through the tree branches, dappling the water. Gray boulders, flecked with mineral sparkles, surrounded most of the pool. On the far shore there was a small sandy beach, and beyond that, a patch of meadow filled with sunshine-yellow buttercups and cool lavender forget-me-nots. The pool itself was clear and brilliant green.

I laid back on a flat boulder, closed my eyes, and listened. Skittering critters. Swishing branches. Singing birds.

I began to feel like a cat, studying the forest with my eyes closed, using just my ears and nose. The swampy green smell of the pool's edges. The dusky dry smell of the tree branches in summer. The cold mineral smell of the stone upon which I laid.

After a while I felt as if I were dreaming this magic place.

But that tiny lapping sound wasn't a dream.

I lifted my head until I could see the pool. The water was no longer still. Ripples, concentric circles of miniature waves, rolled toward me. Then I saw what was making the ripples.

A cougar stood on the sandy beach, its head dipped to the water, drinking. Her tail hung low, all except for the black tip which she held off the ground. Her front legs were bent as she crouched by the pool's edge, her black and white muzzle at the water, and her great pink tongue lapping.

Suddenly her ears shot straight up. She stopped drinking, but didn't lift her head. She held herself perfectly still, listening. I did the same.

Then all at once she lifted her head and looked directly at me.

Make yourself big, my books said. Slowly I rose from my hideout behind the boulders, to let her know what I was, to keep her from having to investigate me.

As I rose, I saw two kittens, stepping from the shadows behind her into the sunlight. They had bright blue eyes, and their tawny coats were covered with silly black spots. The kittens' muzzles were white with black outlines.

One of the kittens stepped forward and hissed. The mother cougar glanced over her shoulder at the hissing little furball. This was the most dangerous situation of all: encountering a mother with kittens. I should shout and wave my arms. I should pick up rocks and hurl them at her. That's what the books said to do.

But I didn't do it. Not because I wasn't scared. I *was* scared. I knew she could kill me in about five seconds. But somehow, as frightened as I felt, I also knew she *wouldn't* kill me.

Maybe I was wrong, though. The big female took a step toward me, as if she were getting ready to come around to my side of the pool.

One of her kittens hissed again, and she looked back at it. Suddenly she sprung about and trotted toward her two offspring, hustling them back into the woods. Only when she reached the edge of the shade, before she disappeared into its darkness, did she turn to look at me one last time.

It was like my dream, me and the cougar looking at each other. I hoped that she stayed down here in the deepest part of the canyon. I hoped she didn't go where she might scare people. I stared for a long time at the dark shadow into which she disappeared.

So this was the pool Sam had meant! He also had been right about there being more than one cougar. It all made sense now. The territories of females sometimes overlapped with those of males.

And of course the kittens would be with their mother. Sam had been right about everything, at least as far as the cougars went.

When I got back to the Muir picnic area, I didn't rejoin my family right away. Soon I would tell them about the mountain lion family. I knew they would keep the secret. But for just a few minutes I wanted to have the mother cougar and her kittens all to myself. I lay down in the grass and looked up into the wide open blue sky, as if it too were part of my destiny. What next? I asked the sky. What next?